VANESSA SPENC
She was named afte[...]
who was her great aunt. She grew up in Jamaica and was later
educated at the Universities of Oxford and Yale. She has lived
in Sierra Leone, India and Pakistan and travelled widely in
East and Southern Africa. As an economist, she has worked in
the fields of public utility regulation and development banking.
She now works for the state privatisation agency in Kingston
and lives in the Blue Mountains. *The Roads Are Down* is her first
novel.

VANESSA SPENCE

The Roads Are Down

HEINEMANN

Heinemann Educational
A Division of Heinemann Publishers (Oxford) Ltd
Halley Court, Jordan Hill, Oxford OX2 8EJ

Heinemann: A Division of Reed Publishing (USA) Inc.
361 Hanover Street, Portsmouth, NH 03801-3912, USA

Heinemann Educational Books (Nigeria) Ltd
PMB 5205, Ibadan
Heinemann Educational Boleswa
PO Box 10103, Village Post Office, Gaborone, Botswana

FLORENCE   PRAGUE   PARIS   MADRID
ATHENS   CHICAGO   MELBOURNE   JOHANNESBURG
AUCKLAND   SINGAPORE   TOKYO   SAO PAULO

First published by Heinemann International Literature and Textbooks
in 1993

Series Editor: Adewale Maja-Pearce

British Library Cataloguing in Publication Data
A catalogue record for this book is available from the British Library.

ISBN 0435989308

Cover design by Touchpaper
Cover illustration by Rosemary Woods

Photypeset by
Wilmaset Ltd, Birkenhead, Wirral
Printed and bound in Great Britain
by Cox & Wyman Ltd, Reading, Berkshire

93 94 10 9 8 7 6 5 4 3 2 1

Katherine

When I was driving up the hill today I hit a child, a boy of about
seven. He didn't seem to be badly hurt, I'd knocked him over with
the left edge of my front bumper, taking a corner too sharply.
Before I could get out of the car he had limped down the hillside
and hidden in the bush, like an animal. I shouted. I tried to find
him and wandered around in the guinea grass under the young
mango trees. I yelled reassurance. But there was no sign of him.
Eventually I just got back into my car and drove home, thinking of
the way he had hugged his ribs as he limped off. He will describe
the car, he will describe me. If he has parents or family to tell. This
area is so small that I will be easily identified. Nowadays I don't
try to avoid what is coming to me, although escaping the
consequences has always been one of my main preoccupations. I
can no longer tell whether I've gotten away, or if I'm ever free and
clear. I sat on the verandah and held my daughter in my arms, and
prayed for rain.

*

Some time ago I was living in a small wooden house way up in the
St Andrew hills. From such a distance, the diesel fumes and the
noise and poverty unto death of Kingston are reduced to a hazy
view of plain white buildings spread among the green trees that
clothe and soften the city. Kingston, ringed by mountains, runs
smoothly into the harbour and the wild blue horizon. From such a
distance, the city can be almost overlooked.

The house was in a district which is generally thought of as part

1

of the coffee-growing region of the Blue Mountains, but most of the coffee is grown much higher up, in the more inaccessible valleys and mountain sides of Portland and St Thomas. I had a few coffee trees in my garden. They were never tended properly and they demonstrated, fairly comprehensively, the damage which could be caused by the berry borer and leaf rust.

I was born up in the hills, and unless you love the old forests near the mountain peaks and the sight of shadowy blue slopes falling to the sea, there is not much incentive to live where the advent of either the rainy season (May, June, October), or the hurricane season (June to October), or the dry season (July, August) can be a serious inconvenience. But there is nothing like worrying about water, electricity and roads to keep your mind off murder and sex, and politics and competition. For a long time after I moved up there, my main activity was to check my water tank for dogs, frogs, and other signs of life.

In the mornings when I drove down to work I passed the battered old Land Rovers of the smallholders – the people who cultivated twenty or thirty acres in the Blue Mountains – racing up the road, a good half an hour before the young, smiling farm managers from the big plantations passed me in their new Land Cruisers. They all drove fast, risking themselves and me, on the hairpin bends and blind corners that joined together to make the road up the hill.

How long had it been since the people who ran the plantations went to live in Kingston? I knew the old owners still lived up there, where they could watch the erosion and the bush fires turning forests and coffee estates into skellion patches.

I rarely saw any of my middle-class neighbours. They were mostly business people or professionals who worked for themselves, and probably aspired never to work at all. They were up, and off the hill, before I struggled out of bed, and they were all back home long before I was, with their children and their six-thirty dinners.

After finishing work in Kingston I used to go and have a few drinks with my friends, and by the time I was going home I was more likely to meet the huge logging trucks belonging to Forest

Industries, parked, without lights, across the dark road. They were not supposed to take the timber out during the day because they were an added hazard to traffic on the narrow hill roads. So they worked at night, and people like me who were not at home at a respectable hour would just have to wait until they were good and ready to move out of the way.

At that time I was quite happy with the way things were. Although I didn't know any of my middle-class neighbours, I did know all the poorer ones – the women who picked the coffee in season and the women that sorted the beans in the coffee factory, the *obeah* man, the small farmers who grew skellion and carrots, the ones that had five acres of coffee, the people that ran the little bars and shops, the men that worked on the roads and the men that worked for the water commission. They were mostly natives of the area and lived close enough to Kingston to be glad – like me – that they did not live in it. The ones that didn't long for Portland and old time plenty, longed for America.

I gave these people lifts up and down the hill every day. I called it 'being part of the community'. I took their mothers to the bus stations downtown, and their children to hospital. I liked them. They were not simple people but they were prepared to be that way for me. We talked about the weather and growing Irish potatoes, 'horse dead and cow fat'. Only very occasionally would anyone venture a 'Ah get problems, ma'am,' and tell me about having to lock shop, look work, leave man, beat pickney, run from police.

As I remember, it was the rainy season when I met them. It had been raining steadily for about two weeks. Every morning and afternoon it would rain for a couple of hours. The roads in Kingston would be virtually impassable after half an hour of rain. It had always been that way. Some of the roads were built in the beds of dry rivers, and where a river has once gone it will always try to go again. In Kingston, in the rainy season, the rivers could go exploring.

The drains were choked full of rubbish and the gullies could not carry the water away fast enough. Cars broke down in the middle of Hope Road and in the side streets off the main roads old cars

3

were abandoned for days. It was a common sight to see people clambering on top of their vehicles after they had hazarded a particularly deep stretch of water, and their cars flooded while they were fighting with the gears.

My boss, Richard, told us that if we got stuck in the rain at lunch-time we were not to try to get back to the office; instead we should wait where we were until the water had gone down a little. Naturally we all began taking three-hour lunches, or, on some occasions, never going back to the office at all, once we had found a nice dry bar somewhere.

It was one of those afternoons when it had rained constantly, the sky had been overcast for the past week and we were getting tired of the English light and of wet shoes and damp hair. I had gone for lunch with a friend, and we'd stayed at the restaurant, drinking coffee and then rum until about five o'clock. I was looking forward to getting home to my little house and going to bed with a book. The nice thing about the wet season in the mountains is the cold. You can wrap yourself up in pyjamas and quilts and sleep long and deeply every night.

I was half-way up the hill that evening, and nervous because it was nearly dark and the mist was coming down and I had noticed several small landslides and branches lying in the road. I came around the corner just beyond Dublin Castle and there was a jeep and a small truck in front of me and a huge landslide right across the road. The pile of mud and earth was six feet high and a large old mango tree was still upright in the middle of it. I could see a mass of huge gnarled mango roots spreading out from the mud and rock so that you could not even get near the edge of the slide.

There was no one standing on the road or digging or anything. I knew it had just come down, because normally a blocked road would bring out every man jack in those hills. I parked behind the jeep and jumped out, and men got out of the jeep and the truck at the same time.

The truck driver stood there shaking his head. 'Bwoy, is God save me tonight. Is jus' as I slow down pon' dis corner I see dat tree moving and I say, mek me stop. Mek me jus' hol' on one minute.

4

Then I jus' see the whole road come down in me face. Lawd have mercy.'

The other man, white, middle-aged, American, wearing a suit, was more excited than thankful. His vehicle had not been in danger of being buried in mud. 'That thing came down so fast, it was incredible. Like an avalanche.'

I could tell from his excitement that he was a stranger in the area, so I offered him the benefit of my experience.

'It's the season,' I told him. 'It's because it's been raining for weeks and the ground is soaked, and there aren't enough trees left to hold the soil.'

He didn't seem impressed, and I turned my attention to the truck driver who had already got over his narrow escape and was wondering whether the landslide would be cleared tonight or whether he was going to have to leave the truck, which, apparently, he was more than willing to do. Lights appeared on the other side of the landslide and then four boys came over the top, treading on stones and branches to avoid sinking in the mud. I recognised one of them – he was building a house out of cut stone for one of the farmers in Mavis Bank.

I waved to him. 'Roy, I hope you bring your shovel. I don't feel to sleep on the road tonight.'

Roy laughed and came bounding down, hopscotching over the roots. 'Evening, ma'am,' he said. 'Anybody gone to tell PWD in Gordon Town?'

'It jus' come down. Jus' now,' the truck driver told him. We went into consultation, pointedly excluding the white man as a stranger and a foreigner – he was definitely American – from our deliberations. But he didn't go away. He stood there smiling and listening to us, as though we were a bunch of experts. I thought perhaps he was some sort of development official. He looked as though he was waiting to hear something he could reinforce.

It was completely dark now and the mist had come down and covered us. The road behind had vanished and it was cold, cold, cold. Nobody wanted to go back to Gordon Town for the PWD. Up in those parts they were usually very conscientious, but we all had the feeling that nobody would come out tonight to clear the road. The influential people who lived up this way – the ones who rated instant attention from the PWD – had probably passed this point already, and the slide was too big to clear without a bulldozer. We spent a few minutes reassuring each other that it wasn't our responsibility.

The boys from Mavis Bank had been going to town to collect cement for tomorrow, but they didn't mind if they didn't get it. The past week it had been too wet to work anyway. The truck driver decided to turn and go back to town. He would report the landslide, but he would not wait around to see if it was going to be cleared. The boys from Mavis Bank could give me a lift home. We were all all right, no worries.

As the American was still standing there, I turned to him and asked very politely if they – there was a woman in the car who had not stirred out of it all this time – would be able to get to their destination.

'Oh, that's not a problem,' he said. 'I guess we can always walk home. It's only a couple of miles.'

This seemed to me a rather uncomfortable proposition for a portly man in a suit and glasses wet from the mist but I didn't comment. If he wanted to walk home – uphill in the dark, along these narrow roads in the mist – he could.

While Roy was offering them a ride in the back of the pick-up, I calculated that they must be living at the Porters' house up the old Flamstead road. It was the only house of any size between here and Mavis Bank whose occupants I did not know, or know of. It had been empty for a long time, and I often went up there to look around it. If I'd had the money it's where I would have lived – built about twenty-five years before, it was concrete but finished with wood. The gardens were enormous, they had a ten-thousand gallon water tank, a beautiful view, and best of all, to my mind, there were deep verandahs running along three sides of the house.

When I was a child, before the Porters moved to America, I had been there a few times with my mother. They had all their furniture on the verandahs – sofas, chairs, bookcases, beds, hammocks, dining table, desk. The Porters went inside only to bathe and to cook. Their children slept in bunk beds near the

6

living room door, and the end of one verandah was screened off and there Mr and Mrs Porter had their double bed. At six, this became my ideal life. To wake in the morning to the smell of the honeysuckle that grew all over the verandah railings and to see the dark blue peaks of the mountains at Portland Gap.

I realised I was staring fixedly at the American while I saw verandahs in my mind's eye, but he was not perturbed. He was asking Roy what was the name of the store on the corner a little further up. Roy was not sure what the man was talking about.

'He means the bar at Goat Corner,' I translated, 'Foxy's Hideaway.' It was not really called Goat Corner, it was just where I had once hit one of the goats that slept on that spot of warm tarmac after dark.

'Well, can I invite you guys to join me for a drink at Foxy's Hideaway? It's so cold. I need a drink to warm me up.'

The others waited for me to say something to indicate that the invitation was meant for me, the only obviously middle-class person there. The man was looking directly at Roy, so I said, 'Thanks,' for all of us.

Roy and his friends adapted more quickly that I did to this departure from our foreign-white-man-type. They told him how to turn his jeep, and where to park it, so that it would be safe till morning, and out of the way of the bulldozer when it came. By the time I had reversed slowly down the road through the mist to the bank above Mrs John's house, and stumbled down her muddy path to beg one of her sons to keep an eye on the car for me, I was very cold and miserable. I picked my way across the landslide, clutching my shopping. The pick-up was gone – only as far as Foxy's Hideaway, I was sure, but it still annoyed me that they hadn't waited.

There were men coming down the road. They had heard about the landslide and were going to inspect it. In another half an hour the place would be full of people. I bade them goodnight, but didn't answer any of their questions.

At Foxy's Hideaway there were ten or twelve men standing around and a few children waiting patiently to buy matches or sardines or flour from the shelves behind the counter. No one was

7

in a hurry to leave the light and dry roof to go back out on to the wet dark hill. The Americans were occupying the only two bar stools. The wife was much younger than her husband. She might have been in her late thirties while he might have been pushing sixty. She looked uncomfortable sitting there in a country bar which was also the local shop. The drivers and farmers in their dirty workclothes and broken shoes were doubtful as to what they were supposed to do – most of them were being friendly, which was what I thought was making her uncomfortable. She couldn't catch the comments and questions bubbling around her.

The man got off the stool as I came in and dumped my shopping with exaggerated weariness.

'Sit down here. What can I get you? Oh, by the way, I'm Bob and this is my wife, Sandy.' Sandy forced a smile. She seemed nearly as tired as I was. Bob, on the other hand, seemed so happy to see me I almost cheered up and made an effort to be sociable.

'I'd like an Appleton, thank you. The dark rum. I'm Katherine.'

Bob was already on good terms with the young man behind the bar, and they were telling each other jokes about how to keep warm on cold nights.

'Are you living at the Porters' house?' I asked Sandy.

'Yes, we just moved in at the weekend. We knew the Porters in the States.'

'Oh, well, welcome to Jamaica. You'll soon get used to this sort of thing. In the rainy season it happens every fortnight. It's a good way to meet the neighbours.'

She made an effort to look happy at the prospect, and said, 'I just wish we had some closer neighbours. I worry about the security up here.' She looked around, smiling at the bar full of potential petty thieves and murderers. She had probably never been this close to people who lived on less than a thousandth of her income. But she looked as though she would soon get used to it, abandon fear for envy, and fix her eyes on the ones that had a thousand times more. In general, I liked the foreigners that were less shocked but didn't get used to it. I wondered how Sandy would classify Ruby, who I knew lived in a little one-room shack on the road to the Porters' – probably not as a neighbour.

8

'Oh, you just need to get to know some more of the local people,' I said, copying her ingenuous smile. 'Then you won't feel so isolated.'

Bob caught the word 'isolated', and put an arm around his wife, handing me the glass of rum that had been sitting on the bar, waiting for the bartender to get to the punch line.

'We were pretty surprised at how far the house is from Kingston. Mrs Porter told me it was a great location,' he said.

I laughed, and because I didn't like Sandy's complaining face, I said, 'Well, to Mrs Porter it was a great location. She raised five children there, she grew strawberries, she made goat's cheese, she had a famous herb garden, she gave these enormous weekend parties and barbecued chickens for a hundred people. You should have seen that house on Saturday mornings. Three people from the French Embassy trying to buy cheese and tarragon, buyers from the hotels fighting each other over who was going to get the strawberries, a truck full of chairs for the party stuck in the driveway, and Mrs Porter would be rushing around telling everybody to shut up. Mr Porter always maintained that his business was just a sideline – Mrs Porter's businesses were what supported the family.'

Sandy took these remarks in the spirit in which they were intended and looked irritated, but Bob was interested in the idea. 'Did she really ever make money off that stuff? The strawberries?'

'I don't know,' I conceded. 'I was very little. But I remember the shadehouses – there were four big shadehouses where they grew the strawberries, and there was a shed – that's still there – where they packed them. And you used to be able to buy them in the supermarket – Blue Mountain strawberries in little baskets. And I remember asking my mother to buy some of the goat's cheese, and her saying that Mrs Porter charged diplomat's prices, and only the ambassadors bought it.'

'There you go, honey. We'll set you up in the strawberry business,' Bob said cheerfully, squeezing her shoulder. 'You'll make a million and I can retire.'

'You don't want to retire. And I don't want to grow strawberries.' She gave him a kiss and I looked away.

Despite the generosity with the drinks, the thought of them living at the Porters and not liking it, was annoying. I abandoned a vague plan to go and visit them there to see what they had done with the house. I got off the stool, saying, 'It's really not the life for everyone up here. In the rainy season the roads collapse, and in the dry season there's no water. You'd probably be better off looking for a townhouse in Kingston and letting the Porters place to someone that wants to live up here in Back of Behind Cow.'

I excused myself while they laughed, and went to bully Roy into finishing his drink and taking me home. Some more men came in with the news that a power line was down somewhere and there was no light in Mavis Bank. Bob and Sandy decided to go back to Kingston to spend the night, and we all departed hurriedly as it began to rain.

That was the first time I met them. I was disappointed that I didn't see them again on the road. It would have amused me to hear how they were managing. Eventually I heard from their invisible neighbours – the security risks that lived in a little house half a mile from the Porters – that they had moved out. The agent for the Porters came to my office one day on some other business. I asked him what had happened to the Americans.

'Oh, it was too isolated for the wife. You know these Americans – they want people all round them. They got themselves a place in one of those complexes in Liguanea.'

'Yes, I met them one night at a landslide and I could see she wasn't cut out for the life up there.' Bob, on the other hand, had seemed interested in meeting the locals.

'Well, the Porters kind of pushed them into taking the house. After they'd been in there two weeks it turned out that rats had eaten away most of the floorboards in the kitchen, and all the pipes were so rusty the water was brown. Kind of thing you don't notice on a quick visit.' He absolved himself of responsibility. 'But they paid three months' rent although they weren't in there more than two at the most. Nice people. Most of those Americans would have been fighting you for their money back after the first time they saw a rat. By the way, are you interested in the house? Now the Porters are having to spend some money on it, they see how it might be better to have somebody there, looking after the place, even if they're not getting a high rent.'

I looked at him and started jumping up and down. The other people who were still lingering in the room after the end of the meeting, laughed. 'I've always wanted to live in that house. Always. Always.'

I got the house strictly on their terms. If they found someone who would pay more rent I would get three months' notice to get out. But I would be paying the same rent as in my little bungalow, and a sleepy and limitless hope of living, not just like the Porters, but at the Porters, was realised.

I also knew that the Porters, getting old and rich in Washington, probably never thought about the house more than twice a year. As for the agent, he would be only too glad not to have to drive up the winding roads into the hills every few months to check that the house was still standing. Once in, I might be there until a will was read. Tomorrow or in twenty years.

My helper, Louise, who was living with her children in Guava Ridge in one room with two other families, was ecstatic. The Porters had a three-room maid's quarters behind the house, complete with toilet and shower, and an enclosed kitchen – something she had never had. Desmond, the agent, said something about the old lady who had worked for the Porters and for most of the previous tenants. I refused to take her with the house. She hadn't lived on the premises anyway, and Louise was my security. Born and bred in the western part of the island, she was a stranger in the hills, and, like me, she liked and distrusted the people around us. She slept with a machete under her bed, and I had once taken her boyfriend to casualty at the University Hospital, so I knew she could use it.

The day after I got the keys Louise moved in. Her friends carried her belongings two miles down the road on their heads, and when I stopped there on the way home, there was a party going on.

She showed me around proudly. Her rooms had been minimally

furnished with cast-offs from the house. As Mrs Porter had been, and probably still was, a generous woman, there was nothing there that was broken or filthy, only worn or chipped. The walls were still bare but I knew it was only a matter of days before old calendars and magazine pictures would adorn them. What caught my attention was my rubbish displayed by Louise's children on the shelves in the kitchen. Old ballpoint pens, tissue cartons, special bottles of nasal drops, a diary from my insurance company – they had all been carefully picked out of the rubbish before it was burnt.

'Well, I tell you what, let's go into the house now and see if we can't find you some pictures and little tables and things. And you should really make the children throw away some of their junk. It's just cluttering up the place,' I said, stepping over Louise's friends who were also cluttering up the place. My arrival had subdued them all but they were prepared to wait for the employer, the missis, to leave so they could resume their party.

Louise's friends did not only know me as the lady who gave lifts up and down the hill. They knew me as the lady who didn't want any radios playing near the house when she was home at the weekends, who would shout and scream and carry on badly if she found out that Louise had lent them any garden tools, or worse, kitchen cutlery or screwdrivers. Now they were suitably respectful and resentful.

We found the keys and went into the main house. Louise had taken time during the day to start cleaning, and she knew where all the lights were. I wandered through the house which was as empty and semi-functional as I remembered it. The kitchen had two enormous stoves and yards of blue tiled countertops and no cupboards or shelves. Mrs Porter had kept everything on the countertops, including the cutlery which was all thrown into a basket.

There were two huge bathrooms, each with separate showers and baths, sofas, full-length wardrobes and innumerable wooden towel racks for family bathtimes. The bedrooms, designed only to be used by guests or sick children, were featureless, cupboardless, four walls with a bed and windows. In the living room the wicker

chairs, long verandah sofas, tall rickety bookcases, desks like
trestle tables where the little Porters had sat to do their homework
two and three at a time, had the worn look of the furniture in
Louise's room – not so much from use, I realised, but from years
on the verandah only just out of reach of sun and rain.

I took four dull watercolours out of the bathrooms for Louise.
They seemed to be the only pictures in the house. Louise was
telling me her plans for growing red peas, clearing out the packing
shed to store tools, using the old cement barbecues to dry coffee
beans from the trees in the garden.

It was completely dark but we opened the doors and went on to
the front verandah. The verandah seemed vast without the
furniture and children racing along full pelt; a staging post for
visits into the dark garden, through the forest, up the mountain, all
now invisible in the darkness. The honeysuckle was gone, though
it had been here on my last visit several months ago. That was the
only evidence of Bob and Sandy's stay. I could hardly believe
Sandy had spent even eight weeks here, without doing any more
damage than cutting down a vine.

We stood there – Louise and I – and we were both so happy.
There are some places where ghosts have been unable to take hold.
No one had died in that house, the land had never been part of the
coffee estates, there was nothing in that place except Mrs Porter
and her strawberries, and Mr Porter telling stories to his myriad
children. Someone has to be very unhappy somewhere to make a
really good ghost. I was determined to be happy there and so was
Louise. We wouldn't make any ghosts at the Porters, even if it
meant making a few somewhere else.

I borrowed a van from a man in Mavis Bank and moved the next
weekend. I didn't ask any of my friends to help. I felt slightly
embarrassed about the Porters' house. People would understand
about it being in the hills and the remote location bringing down
the rent, but still . . . It was a large house with ten acres of land. It
was not expensive. It was furnished, and the Water Commission
and the power company had not yet extended their efficiency

13

campaigns into these hills. Water was free and electricity bills were based on out-of-date meter readings. My friends were all living in ugly apartments or townhouses in Kingston that devoured most of their salaries, and although they would no more have troubled themselves to live in the hills than I would have accepted living in Kingston, I was wary of their reaction when they saw the size of the house in which I proposed to live alone.

Louise and I spent the day dragging furniture outside and investigating. Louise refused to countenance the idea of me sleeping on the verandah. 'Those days finish and gone,' she said. I ended up putting my clothes in the bathroom wardrobe and shoving a double bed by the window in the front bedroom. I quickly appreciated why Sandy had left the house untouched – the too large rooms and weathered furniture were either the perfect combination or irredeemable without an architect and a stand-by carpenter.

That night I slept for twelve hours, and when I woke up Louise had started a fire on the barbecue and was roasting breadfruit. Her three children were running around the garden shrieking at the tops of their voices. They had never had so much room to play when they were not playing on the road. I sat on the verandah and did nothing except look out at the Blue Mountains and smile to myself.

I was still thinking about nothing in particular and drinking coffee and eating a hot piece of breadfruit when Bob arrived. I heard the jeep in the driveway which approached the other side of the house, but I didn't get up. Louise had left the barbecue and gone around to the front, and I thought maybe it was one of her boyfriends who drove for the Forestry Commission. But in a few seconds Bob came along the verandah proffering a bottle of dark rum. I jumped up, full of embarrassment and belligerence in case he might be wanting to move back up here.

'Hi, Katherine! I met Desmond at a party last night and he told me you were living up here. No wonder you wanted us out!' he said, with what could only be an excess of friendliness and good humour. I couldn't tell whether he was joking or not and I greeted him very formally, which he completely ignored. He danced around, wouldn't sit down, wanted to see what I'd done with each and every room. Irrepressible.

Eventually, after I'd shown him the house, he agreed to sit and drink some rum with me. There is something about a happy man that you can't do anything about. He had twice as much energy as I had on my best days, and he managed to force me into a good humour almost as pervasive as his. I remembered this vaguely from the night on the road and I already felt comfortable enough with him to mention it.

'You really shocked us all, that night at the landslide,' I said. 'Taking us all for a drink. Not the sort of behaviour we expect from American foreigners.' Establishing that people are foreigners and therefore completely different from our multi-racial, multi-cultural selves is an island preoccupation, and one I always do my duty by.

He looked puzzled. 'Is that right? I've seen those guys from the Central American Advisory in just about every bar up here.'

He was right of course. Those Americans were part of a bilateral effort to improve coffee yields and they knew every farmer in the district. They were nice men but they spent time in the country bars because that's what they had done in their frenzied years in fully accredited banana republics. They were boastfully at ease among our farmers who would rarely kill for politics or drugs or even money.

'Those guys aren't foreigners; not like you're a foreigner,' I said unhelpfully. That shut him up for a while, and gave me a chance to wonder why he had chosen to visit. That night on the road I had been too interested in finding my way home and thinking about the house to notice what he was like. He was friendly and open and fleshy, that was all I had gathered.

Louise's eldest girl, Angeline, came up with a plate of roast breadfruit and offered it to us. Bob helped himself with much enthusiasm and then insisted on going to have a look at how it was done. I watched him harassing Louise and the children. He looked much older than he was, judging by the sprightly way he chased the children round the barbecue. He had a worn, deeply wrinkled face, faded hair and all over, the too solid flesh that marks out an

15

American. They seem more real than other white people, even without their possessions. He caught the little one and tossed her in the air, much to the delight of the others. By the time each child had been picked up and whirled around, he was exhausted and struggled back to slump on the verandah sofa. He shook his head at me.

'Those kids are much heavier than they look. I can't do stuff like that any more.'

'You certainly look very tired.' He was suffering, breathing with the anxious and embarrassed expression of a man with a high risk heart. His shirt had pulled nearly out of his trousers and his distress made all his clothes grab and squeeze at his fat. I looked away.

'You haven't told me what brings you up here,' I said. He was breathing more easily and seemed to be aiming big relaxed smiles at my profile.

'You do. I was supposed to be going to the beach this afternoon with some guys from my office. My wife's gone to some bazaar with a friend of hers. But it's too damn hot in Kingston for me, and I thought I'd just come and see how you were up in the nice cool hills.' He paused for a moment, considering whether this was an adequate answer. 'I kind of liked it up here, you know. This is such a great house and the view is just incredible. And it's always so cool up here. I think about it when I'm sitting in that townhouse and I have to put on the air conditioning.' He paused again. 'But I'd hate to have to do that drive every day, and Sandy was just too isolated. She liked it as well, but she just wasn't getting a chance to meet people or anything.'

I looked with some satisfaction at the garden, where the overgrown lawn dotted with old juniper trees dropped down to a steep slope covered in wynne grass and vanished into a forest of juniper and cedar and Norfolk Island pine. Above the tops of the forest rose the peaks of Portland. Everything was in shades of blue and green except the wisps of mist massing on the mountain slopes. In two hours the mist would come down into the valleys and cover everything for the night.

'Have some more rum?' I said to Bob.

We had some rum and he began telling me about his first weeks on the island and how he had felt the shock of being both unknown and unimportant. He described Sandy's reactions to Jamaicans and how quickly she had gone from enthusiasm for the people to irritation and superiority. I listened to him, smiling so much that I had to keep my eyes on the garden to prevent him from thinking I meant appreciation as invitation. It was wonderful to be fed these intimacies by a man I didn't know and to whom I had no obligation. I worried that he was not being careful with himself. Here, confessing that you are afraid of anything other than a gunman with an M-16, will make people's eyes light up as they consider how best to take advantage.

I was very hungry after a while, and he came and sat at the kitchen table while I made us toasted cheese sandwiches. There was, as usual, almost no food in the house. Bob asked me if I had a boyfriend. I said yes, as a matter of course. My friend Carla, who advised me about these things, said you should never indicate to a man, whom you yourself are not interested in, that you are unattached. Always maintain that you are about to marry the most wonderful man in the world, who is not only incredibly good looking but is rich and is either very powerfully built or never goes anywhere without his two evil bodyguards. It's the only way, Carla said. Otherwise, worries. You can be truthful when you're sixty. I told him I had a boyfriend but I liked his old man eyes and his thin mouth.

Bob could talk. He talked and talked. He wanted to know all about Jamaica but interrupted my replies. He told me about his job, or rather about his business. He was part owner of some kind of fisheries operation that supplied fresh frozen seafoods to restaurants on the East Coast, and had come down to the Caribbean for two years to see if there wasn't any way to diversify or boost profits. He had made lots of money but he would like to make more. He promised to send me some fish, and asked where I worked.

It was very relaxing listening to him. I spend a lot of time alone, and at that time, when I was in company, you usually couldn't shut me up. But Bob never gave me a chance to get started. All his

17

stories were very self-deprecating and I could tell that, apart from having a business based on Gulf Stream fishing, he had as narrow a background as any small town American, and he was suffering a little for it in Jamaica. We are cosmopolitan small-islanders; we have fathers from India, mothers from China, aunts in New York, sisters in East Germany, brothers in Ghana, uncles in England. We like everybody and we dislike everybody else. Bob did not know how to cope with apparently friendly people telling him how much they didn't like him.

At seven o'clock Louise came in to say goodnight. We were still sitting on opposite sides of the kitchen table. Bob had been drinking steadily, helping himself to a glass of rum every twenty minutes, and we had long since finished the bottle he had brought with him. I suppose it was the concerned look on Louise's face as she saw the one and a half empty bottles and Bob's face, the features of which had dissolved into a pink mass, that made me remember he was someone I had met for five minutes at a landslide.

'You really should go before it gets too late,' I said, getting up and clearing the glasses, not looking at him. 'Sandy will be worried.'

He got up, and gave a little shrug. 'Sandy's heard all my stories before.'

When he got to his jeep – I had followed him out trying to think of something to say that would both thank him and warn him – he gave me an apologetic smile. 'Hey, sorry I took up your whole afternoon.'

I took a step back and put my arms behind me. 'Oh, no problem. Come up any time you get sick of Kingston. Say hello to Sandy.'

He didn't reply, just got in his shiny new jeep and drove away, looking old, hunched over the steering wheel, peering into the mist.

I felt sorry for him. I called Carla the next day and told her about him, exaggerating, though the truth didn't require it, his age and unattractiveness.

Carla, ever my protector, complained, 'I don't know where you find these people. Me, I keep far from the ones that come down to do business here. You don't know what they want.'

'He just wanted to talk.' I didn't know how to say I liked being talked to like that. All the intimacy, none of the deep demand. I didn't know any men who admitted to being less than one hundred per cent in control at all times.

Carla snorted. She had perfected it when she'd played at being a pig in kindergarten. She thought I was very like a fool, and had stayed friends with me in order to avoid hearing unexpectedly of my horrifying end. Now she asked one of the only two questions she ever asked me about a man.

'What's the wife like?'

'Oh, God, why are you asking me that? I'm not going to have an affair with him,' I protested. A path to the past.

'Who said anything about that? What's she like?'

'She's much younger than him. Like twenty years younger. She seems OK.' I had thought about it last night.

'All right, so he's probably been married before.'

Carla just made these deadpan comments and left them there for someone else to worry about. She was in town planning, in it and consumed by it – and if you called her at work, she had to drag her attention away to talk to you. You could visualise her eyes straying back to the building code.

'So what? I just feel sorry for him. He's old and he just came here and he doesn't know anyone. He was bored. And his wife has heard all his stories.'

Carla laughed. 'He came out with that? Well, at least he's not going to tell you about how his wife doesn't understand him. Maybe he's going to tell you about how his wife understands him too much.' She laughed again. 'Well, don't think it's your business to make his life more interesting. When you're sixty I promise you there won't be any young man to make you feel better about life. It will be you and one old, boring husband. If he isn't dead of a heart attack already. Anyway, see you.' She rang off.

I didn't get any fish, I didn't get any phone calls at work, although the office number was in the book and he knew the name of the company. After several weeks had passed I was still thinking about him, and worrying about how he was dealing with the men that fished the Pedro Banks. Every so often someone would die out there, indeterminately killed by man or sea. I remembered that, after all, he hadn't seemed bored with his life. On the contrary he was brimming with enthusiasm for the world. He enjoyed everything – the landslide, Foxy's Hideaway, my story about the Porters, the breadfruit, the children, the toasted cheese. If he had not been perfectly OK it was because of something else about him: getting old, and being the sort of man who goes to see a woman he doesn't know and delivers a three-hour monologue. Being married and being lonely.

I did see him once, leaving a restaurant just as I was going into it. He was with a group of other middle-aged American businessmen, all pink, all in blue or beige suits, all completely anonymous in a place where the other men had every shade of skin from red to ebony, and were dressed, like peacocks, in all that was bright and fashionable.

It was one-thirty and the Americans were rushing back to their offices, lunch hour over. The Jamaican men, by and large, were ordering more drinks and looking over the few women there. Bob stepped out of the group, which I had glanced at without registering much more than white faces. I was startled when I recognised him. But he just brushed my arm and said, 'Hi, honey,' and kept on going.

'Who was that?' asked the woman I was with. I didn't reply and she forgot to ask me again as she was having a good look round at the possibilities. I thought about him again; he had looked a bit thinner but maybe it was just the suit.

Then Carla found me a boyfriend. She had been alarmed, she said, by anyone being so interested in an old white man. Carla was not particularly racist. She just thought you ought to appreciate the situation in life in which God had placed you. I had been placed as a native of an island where the men were tall and dark and handsome. At parties you could lean against a wall and watch narrow hips and rounded buttocks, lean legs and broad shoulders dancing past you; the faces were made to please, very masculine with big dark eyes, and they all had killer, 'Baby I want you' smiles. They bathed in aftershave and were clean and immaculately dressed. They could dance suggestively, shoving their hips towards you and making slow thrusts that were guaranteed to make you wet your pants. They might be no good as husbands and fathers, but as sexual partners they left nothing to be desired.

You can't have everything, Carla said. Do what our mothers did. When you want to get married go away and find a husband to bring home. You're young, enjoy yourself.

She introduced me to Sam, just back from England. He complained a great deal about Jamaica, and, less directly, about the fact that as a Jamaican he was no longer unique. At his university in England he had stood out, dark skinned, curly haired, golden tongued among the drab, pasty Englishmen. In Jamaica he was no more attractive than anyone else, and girls had a tendency to judge you by your car – he had only been able to afford a VW – and by your prospects. He had good prospects but it was not yet evident what they were.

I suited his needs exactly. I lived in the hills where a VW was an advantage. (BMW owners had to worry about ruining their shock absorbers on my road.) I had been educated in England so I could appreciate his unimaginative comments about their class system and the economy under Thatcher. I was attractive enough to be seen out with, but as I didn't care about being seen, he didn't have to spend much money on me. I lived well, but had even less money than he did.

I couldn't help caring about him, but I didn't care about him very much. I found him to be neither a talker nor a listener, entirely involved in his incomprehensible but concrete plans to become someone. Someone who would have right and access to a more desirable woman than I was. I suspected that on Fridays, and probably on other days in the week as well, Sam was seeing other women, but I didn't ask him in case I couldn't be interested in the answer.

Carla continually congratulated herself on having found Sam for me. 'You look so much better for having some regular sex, and at least you have someone to keep you company on that mountain top.'

Sam did draw me back a little into life in Kingston. I went out more, and instead of drinking in the bars every evening with my friends, I socialised in other ways, and that's how I came to meet Sandy again, several months after Bob had come up to visit me at the Porters.

It was at a garden party for a friend of Sam's in the visa section of the British High Commission. A powerful man in a petty way, there were dozens of people there who had had cause to need his goodwill. Sandy was standing by herself near the drinks table, drinking white wine cooler. I watched her for a little bit before she noticed me and I had to go over and say hello. She was nicely dressed in blue cotton and looked rather voluptuous and glamorous compared to the other white women who were universally in sandals and white dresses that ranged from inappropriate – the very elderly lady in the strapless dress – to awful – the pretty blonde girl in white satin and frills.

Sandy also looked perfectly composed, which I never managed to do when standing alone at a party. Perhaps she was used to it.

'Hi, Katherine. How are you doing?' Her smile was as warm and genuine as her husband's.

'I'm fine. How are you enjoying Jamaica?'

'Oh, I just love it. You have to come by and see us. Bob's been saying we should come up and visit you. Are you still living up there?'

'Oh yes. I have to live in the hills. I can't handle Kingston for very long.'

'It's so pretty up there. Bob would like to get up there more often, but he's just been so busy. They're bringing down a whole bunch of trawlers and he's having problems with the government. Anyway, he reckons everything will be fixed up soon and then he'll be able to spend more time out of the office.'

This seemed to exhaust Sandy's conversational powers and she was edging away, her warm genuine smile glued to her face. I tried to detain her by asking what she did with her time, but having given me to understand that I wouldn't be interested in what she did, she went off to stand by herself in another part of the garden.

A little while later she was joined by another woman and they left immediately.

The next weekend Sam had been invited to Ocho Rios for a party. I didn't go because I hoped that Sandy would have mentioned meeting me and reminded Bob of my existence. In which case he might come to visit. I expected him, although as Carla said, I didn't know what he wanted.

On Saturday I spent the whole day wandering around in the forest, following paths for a while and then turning back. The tracks were made by the people from the villages on the other side of Flamstead driving their goats and donkeys through the forest. Occasionally I bumped into someone – a small boy leading a kid, or an old man riding a mule. Walking by myself in the hills was a meditation, broken now and then by the fear of meeting, or 'bucking up', a gunman coming up into the hills from Bull Bay. Like me, some of them felt safer up here.

I started climbing the slope back to the house about four. I hadn't eaten all day and my prolonged wandering and daydreaming had induced a kind of stupor. I had had too much of what I liked best, solitude and walking in the hills. When I reached the top of the slope and stepped on to the lawn below the house I dropped to the ground and lay on my stomach, intending to rest there until it got dark.

I thought I was almost asleep when I heard footsteps and Bob came and awkwardly sat down beside me. I just turned my head to look at him.

'Hey, you! I've been sitting on your verandah for an hour waiting for you to show up. Your helper isn't there so I couldn't even go into the house and get myself a drink.'

'OK, I can take a hint.' I sat up, and gave him my sweetest smile. 'Hello, you. Let's go and get you a drink. I'm sorry you had to wait.'

'Well, of course you should have stayed home all day just in case I decided to come see you. I finally brought you your fish, you'll be happy to know. Snapper, conch and lobster.'

He got on to his feet more quickly than he had got off them, and offered me his hand. He had become very dark in the sun, a strange brown that looked as if it were beneath, instead of over, the pink. As we walked to the house he asked if I was feeling all right, but otherwise he was very quiet until I gave him a drink.

He said that Sandy had mentioned that she'd seen me. I said how very pretty she had looked that day. He ignored that and went on, 'Do you like the sea at all, Katherine? Or is that a dumb question considering where you live?'

'Oh, I like it. It's just that it can be too hot sometimes, along the coast.' I was about to launch into a detailed description of my favourite parts of the coast – Portland, Alligator Pond, Negril – when he interrupted me.

'Well, I have to go down to Port Esquivel tomorrow and bring back a boat that we need to take out on Monday with one of the trawlers. I was wondering if you'd like to go with me. It's pretty scenic along that part of the coast.'

'Oh, I'd love to,' I said, looking at his square, smooth hands. 'I haven't been on a boat for years, but I only like it if we can keep in sight of land. I can swim but I like to know there's somewhere to swim to.'

He laughed. 'I know what you mean. I'm not overfond of the ocean once you're in the middle of it. I like to leave that to the regular fishermen. Anyway, let's try and leave early, say by six o'clock. Is that OK?'

We agreed to meet at his house the next morning. I didn't ask why Sandy wasn't going with us. Bob had mentioned last time that she was suffering very badly with the heat, and I had stopped myself pointing out that it was always much cooler in the mountains.

I had not spoken to anyone all day, but now Bob was actually here I was dreading the monologue that must be in store. I wanted time to get used to him, large and male, taking up most of the verandah sofa.

He sipped his drink and stayed quiet apparently enjoying the view which was changing while we watched. The sun was setting on the other side of the house, and from where we were the long pink streaks were fading slowly and below them, on the blue peaks, the mist was drifting down fast. The wind was picking up and would probably bring rain later in the evening.

We sat there until it was dark and cold, and my neck was rigid from not moving a muscle in case Bob took it as a signal to start a conversation. He got up eventually and taking our empty glasses, went into the house. He didn't come back, so after a long time I followed him inside. He was sitting in the kitchen, with both elbows on the table, drinking. I sat opposite him, and smiled. 'You wanted to finish the bottle alone this time.'

He looked away. 'I had such a good time here last time. I know I talked my head off, but I haven't talked to anyone like that for ages.' He looked at me quickly and then stared at his glass. 'I thought about you so much for months. But I didn't want to come up again and bother you. I can see that you like to be alone as much as you can, and a guy like me just wants to talk your ear off.'

I didn't know what to say without admitting the obvious – that living alone makes company sweet – but to help him out I got up and started fiddling around the kitchen as if I was going to prepare a meal.

'Anyway, don't let me drink all your rum. Can I get you another drink?' he asked.

'No, thanks. But please have one yourself. Do you know how to cook conch? If you tell me I'll make us some.'

'No, I don't know how to cook conch,' he said with some irritation. 'I don't know how to cook anything. In any case, I should go. I'll see you tomorrow.'

He walked out of the kitchen. I didn't go after him. My manners are not especially good.

The next morning I was up at four and headed to Kingston about five, carrying a flask of hot black coffee and a towel and a bathing suit. Anything else necessary Bob and/or Sandy would have to provide.

I had little difficulty finding the townhouse, their complex was just one of four in the same area, all bearing similar names – Poinciana View, Poinciana Court, Poinciana Mews, Poinciana Gardens. They lived in Poinciana Court where the most luxurious houses were. Bob was outside putting things into the jeep. There was no one else awake in that grey pink dawn, although the birds had been singing for an hour. Poinciana Court probably never woke on Sundays, the residents sleeping off the week in their villas on the north coast.

Bob looked a bit surprised to see me. 'I didn't think you were coming.'

I got out of my car. 'Why not?'

He kept on putting stuff in the jeep. 'Well, after the way I left you . . . '

That seemed to be an intimate way to begin six or eight hours together. 'Well, I'm here. Is Sandy inside? I'll just go and say hello.'

Bob leaned against the car and looked at me. 'I took Sandy to the airport yesterday morning. She's gone to the States for a couple of weeks. That's why I was looking for company. Usually, Sandy comes with me.' His face was innocent of any other motive.

'I see.' In embarrassing moments my English grandmother was all-powerful with her stony glance and her 'I see'. It had an immediate effect on Bob who began shifting around and babbling about coffee in the house. Having regained the advantage I refused the coffee and we set off for Port Esquivel in an uncomfortable silence.

He drove very fast but with precision. I watched carefully to see what berth he gave to children and chickens and goats, but didn't comment. Bob seemed to have acquired a good understanding of the island's motor code. Fast and expensive cars to the fore, old cars to the verge, aggressive and defensive driving by everyone all the time. You had to be able to make constant judgements as to whether the truck overtaking you going down a steep slope was trying to get to Montego Bay in record time, in which case you would be obliged to race him, or whether he simply had no brakes and was thoughtfully trying to save your life.

We didn't speak to each other much the whole day, but the silence was fine once we were on the boat. There was a fisherman called Clovis who came with us. He and Bob looked me over in my swimsuit. I tried looking at them but it was too difficult to imagine

26

being in bed under either Clovis' hard angry face or Bob's mild-eyed one.

Bob and Clovis were preoccupied with steering and charts, and I sunbathed and used the binoculars to watch a herd of sea-cows drifting down the coast. I watched Bob moving around the boat. Here was a man that liked to work, especially under a woman's eye. I liked it. A man that was serious about what he did was a change for me. On the island, at least among my friends, work was just a means to an end, and even if you liked your job, you didn't take it that seriously. We told each other work was an Anglo-American conspiracy, imposed by the IMF on a people that would rather spend the day at the beach. Only the entrepreneurs were serious about their work, and would break their hearts over it. The entrepreneurs and the women with children.

When we docked in Kingston, I sat in the jeep, which somone had driven back from Port Esquivel, for nearly an hour while Bob ran around and signed papers. He was bright and pink and bloated from all the beers he'd drunk on the boat. By the time we drove away from the dock he looked exhausted and distressed.

We went for lunch in an air-conditioned seafood restaurant on the wharf. It was late and there was only one other couple there. I had been waiting all day for him to talk to me.

'So did you enjoy your day, Katherine? You've been very quiet.' It was definitely an accusation.

'Oh, yes. It's been years since I saw sea-cows or spent any time along the coast. But I think we both got very burnt.' I smiled at his deep brown and pink scarlet face. He wasn't appeased.

'Are you always so quiet? I'd have thought you were a woman with plenty to say for yourself.' That annoyed me.

'Well, Americans are famous for unburdening themselves to all and sundry, as though you're all part of a global talk-show. But it's purely cultural, as I'm sure you realise. Most people in the world aren't in the habit of sharing their life stories except with their close friends or spouses. They think there are more interesting things to talk about. You know, art, politics, religion, sex. The weather.' I nearly laughed at him, although he was serious, wrinkling his face.

Then he smiled. Now that he had provoked me. 'OK, why don't you just accept my cultural limitations, and tell me your life story? I'm sure if I were a Muslim you wouldn't expect me to sit here and eat pork because you were having some, would you?'

'Not at all. But what kind of example is that? I'm not American so why should I behave like one just because I'm with you?'

'No reason.' He was grinning. 'Tell me your life story anyway.'

'Maybe we should have a conversation about something else.' I put the emphasis on 'conversation' and to labour the point, I added, 'I'm not crazy about monologues.'

His face darkened. 'Is it that you think I'm too dumb to pick up on these comments, or are you just trying to be nasty?'

'Trying? I'm perfectly capable of being very nasty without any effort at all.' I said this casually, looking around the room.

'I'm sure you are.' Bob decided to leave well enough alone, and picked up the menu. 'Let's see what they have.'

'I'm not hungry,' I said.

I could not give it up once my adrenalin had got going. I wanted to amuse myself, and see if I could outdo him in a quarrel without getting angry. I didn't see why Bob should decide how and what we were going to talk about.

'Well, how about having a few drinks and some ice cream and maybe the fruit? That won't be very much to eat but it would kind of cool you down.' He was calm and solicitous. I allowed him to order me an iced drink and chocolate ice cream and fresh chilled mango, and he ordered a very elaborate three-course meal for himself. I could see we were settled in the place for a good two and a half hours at the outside, and that any flesh he might have dissolved during the morning was going to be safely restored in the course of the afternoon. At least the place was air-conditioned so he was gradually losing his just-boiled look.

'What should we converse about, madam?'

'Why not let's have *your* life story?' I wanted to add 'again', but I thought it would be too vicious as an opening remark. He heard it anyway. He just looked tired now, and concerned.

'I apologise for "unburdening" myself the first time I came up to your house. I promise to overcome this grave cultural defect. I hope that you'll be able to forgive my occasionally being influenced by the fifty years I've spent living in America. OK?' He smiled at me, and I had to smile back.

'OK.'

'Good, so now lay off.' He settled back in his chair. A truce. We sat there in silence, while I tried to think of a neutral topic.

'I met your friend Carla the other day,' he said. Carla hadn't mentioned it to me. 'She was waiting to see the Minister of the Environment. We got talking, and I told her where we'd lived when we first came out here. She said she had a girlfriend living up there. So I guessed it must be you. She seems like a nice lady.'

'Oh, she is. We've been friends since kindergarten.'

'That's nice. I've always moved around so much, I wouldn't even know where to go to see someone I went to kindergarten with. Anyway, we both waited for over an hour to see the Minister, and then he had to go out to open something. That was a pain in the ass. So we went and had lunch. She said you weren't too happy with your job right now.'

I was busy trying to think of what day they could have had lunch. It must have been Friday because I'd talked to Carla on Thrusday morning.

'Well, I'm not crazy about it,' I said. 'I work with lots of weird people and I don't really fit in that well. They're so different from me that I spend most of the day trying to understand what's going on in the office.'

'You mean, in terms of the work that's being done?'

'Not really. I don't have any problems with my actual design work. All we do is build these disgusting things all over the north coast, but you know I'm only the engineer. It doesn't bother me really. I just avert my eyes when I drive past one of those estates.' We both laughed. 'It's the people I work with. You know I'm very pragmatic and slow. And they're not like that at all.' I was exaggerating, running myself down, because that's what he did.

He was listening to every word, paying no attention to his oysters which had just arrived.

'For instance, we were all in a meeting last year. We're making a presentation to a client on a new hotel. The client is looking at the plans and he turns to my boss, Richard, and says "Maybe you'd like to explain to us your concept for the giraffe bar". And Richard has a fit, comes forward, looks at the plans and sees that right there in one end of the swimming pool is a neat little drawing of a giraffe and underneath it's printed, GIRAFFE BAR. So of course Richard turns to Rose, who is the chief architect on the project, and says "Well, maybe Rose would like to explain it to you". And Rose just comes up with some bullshit off the top of her head and the client loves it. I think she told him she had seen one like it in Florida.

'What's happend is that at three o'clock in the morning – which is when Rose likes to work – she got a little bit too heavily into her ganja and her Red Stripe and had a bright idea for this giraffe bar in the pool. Anyway, the client leaves and Richard goes nuts and tells Rose to take her goddamn giraffe off his goddamn plans. Rose goes away and thinks about it, and decides maybe she's been working a little too hard, and two days later she takes off for six weeks in Europe. Richard goes home and has a quarrel with his wife, and decides to take his secretary to California for a week.

'OK. Now one of the junior architects gets stuck with the plans. And, as far as I can see, that's how it happens, that last week, when Rose is telling me that she's just about due for another holiday, and Richard's secretary is having hysterics because his wife is always rude to her on the phone, the outside contractor is wandering round the office saying he's starting construction tomorrow and where are the detailed drawings for this bar in the pool? Because, of course, they were never done. That's what I think happened. But I can promise you if I go and ask Richard or Rose they'll give me some entirely different version of events.'

Bob laughed. 'Well, you won't be bored there, anyway. What happened about the bar in the end?'

'Oh, they just took it off the plans, and hoped the client wouldn't ask any questions they couldn't answer. And they always have an answer – which is usually that the engineer said there were going to be problems in construction.' This was not quite true, but it made him laugh again.

'Well, why don't you change your job?'

'I don't know. I'm lazy, I suppose. And as you say, it's not boring. Although I complain about the people, they are a lot of fun to work with. They don't work very much but they're really professional when they do. And we do, very occasionally, get to work on some interesting projects.' I was babbling.

Bob shrugged and gave me a warm look. He appreciated my stories.

That's how we came to be friends. Very easy, very careless.

Carla

The thing about this affair between Katherine and Bob, quite apart from the child, was how many people dragged themselves into it in the end. Dozens of people decided to take a personal interest and then took sides. Katherine didn't even think in terms of whether or not she wanted Bob on a permanent basis. She wanted to go a certain way with him, and then go and do something else with her time. When nearly everybody, except for me, mixed themselves up in her business and then took Bob's 'side', she was angry. She wanted to explain herself. She didn't understand that nobody really cared whether or not there were two ways of looking at that particular issue. People still think she was completely wrong. Completely out of order.

Well, I didn't take his side. I didn't agree with Katherine either. But I liked how hard-hearted she was about the whole thing. She just pretended that she wasn't young, that she wasn't struggling, that, instead, she was old and powerful and weary and knew what there was to know. She just pretended that she'd indulged the world, and no one could ask her for anything any more. Especially not the kind of things Bob was asking for. Katherine likes to live as much as possible as if she's always at the end, and never at the beginning, of anything.

Anyway, the robbery. The beginning of Katherine realising that she didn't want to be part of anything, to be the cause of anything.

You know how it is here. Especially if you live in a rural area. Katherine was always taking people up and down the hill. She liked to do these favours for all these small people living round her. Playing the big lady. Living in the love of the common people, and

33

so forth. So when Bob took to going up there to see her all the time he would give lifts to people as well. In no time at all everyone got to know that the American was the man for the lady at the Porters. Since she was living in a big house and had a white man come to visit her all the time, she was obviously rich; a rich, nice lady. Just who we all want living in our area.

I remember her coming to tell me that she didn't know what to do. Gradually, gradually, it got to be that there would be five or six people coming every day to see her. They would all be waiting when she got home from work. One had a child in hospital, one had hurt himself working in the coffee and hadn't received compensation and couldn't work any more, this one's mother was sick. They didn't just come to her for money, they wanted all kinds of things, all kinds of help. The kind of help you only need to be middle class to give.

First of all, they just wanted her to be 'sorry to hear' about their troubles. Next thing she knew she was going to hospitals to argue with doctors about the treatment they were giving their patients; she was writing letters to the Coffee Board about conditions on the estates; she was going to funerals and wakes almost every week. She was 'talking to' pregnant schoolgirls . . . all this sort of thing.

After a while Katherine established some sort of control over the process. She used to see everyone on Saturday mornings – between ten and twelve. Like an MP's surgery. Sometimes she would see twenty people. When it all started she really didn't have much to offer. She didn't have many contacts, she couldn't get people jobs, she didn't even understand how things worked in Jamaica. You know, like who has influence and who doesn't. Who could be relied upon to keep their promises, and who would promise you anything just to get you out of their office. But after a few months, she actually became very effective in trying to help people and make things a bit better up there in the hills.

Bob, of course, got involved. I think at first it really annoyed him. He thought she was letting herself be taken advantage of. But Bob had a lot of what Katherine didn't have. Through his business he had a lot of government contacts, he had money and he had management experience of dealing with Jamaicans. Little by little, through wanting to help Katherine and to be around her, and through being the sort of man that is basically interested in everything and anything, especially anything to do with people, he was embroiled. We used to call them BMW – Blue Mountain Welfare, because they were such expensive social workers.

Of course, Bob was happy to have an excuse to spend so much time in the hills. He wasn't sleeping with Katherine then. Katherine kept believing that she was somehow going to become friends with Sandy, as well as with Bob, and that she wasn't going to be so stupid as to fall in love with an old married import (that's what we used to call the ex-pats, 'imports').

It was such a long game for that man. About seven or eight months long. But he had the patience to play it. That's why she got caught, and then had to be so careful about getting away. He made himself her friend, then her lover. It was only when it came to the husband part that she woke up and realised what was happening. That the mountain woman, secure and alone, going to Kingston to make her living and drifting around doing exactly what she wanted, could end up as a housewife in Virginia, baking cakes and waiting for her husband to come home. Or even worse, working in some consultancy in D.C. and rushing home to cook dinner and put the kids to bed. The one option was seriously dull, and the other one seemed like far too much hard work.

Katherine reckons that love is just another economic variable. Too much emphasis on any one variable distorts the whole economy. She says her life is a mixed economy – a little planning, a lot left to market forces. Bob or any other husband would introduce too much central planning, and even the best centrally-planned economies eventually become severely distorted, and you have to rush around trying to come up with new policies to deal with these massive problems. Whereas in a mixed economy you retain a certain amount of choice, and you tend not to be obsessed with the idea of determining what happens in the long run.

Katherine has this very backward view, that too much emphasis on love is just an invitation to a whole lot of rules and regulations, time checks and full employment. That's her explanation for being just as afraid as everyone else.

Bob would be up at her house all day Saturday, then on Sundays, they'd go to the beach; one of those black sand beaches out in St Thomas where you drive through the bush to the sea and where you have a whole mile of beach to yourself. They used to have lunch together at least twice a week. Katherine was almost his whole social life. Who knows what his wife thought of it all? We heard what she thought later, but at the beginning she didn't seem to care, or even to be worried about it. Maybe she was really tired of his stories, and was glad not to have to listen to him that much any more.

I did ask him once, what she thought, but he just shrugged and said they didn't talk about it. He was just gone every Saturday and every Sunday and she knew he was with Katherine. Still, I thought it was strange. After all, Sandy was completely dependent on the man. Sandy was either prescient or she didn't give a damn. Either way, it was brave of her, I think. That long period of doing nothing.

Anyway, I think Bob changed his mind about all this platonic friendship business quite quickly, but Katherine didn't. It was only after she was robbed and Bob's time in Jamaica was coming to an end that they actually started going to bed together. Having an affair, although I don't know what you call what they were doing before then. That was a pretty serious friendship. Every Saturday, every Sunday.

I suppose that she took a long time to get rid of Sam, although when she did, it really made no difference. He had another girlfriend in a day, and Bob had already been around for months. I think she felt Sam was a good insurance against having an affair with Bob. Actually that's what I kept telling her.

The robbery really changed the dream. There was Katherine in her mountain house, completely involved in the community up there, and, as we thought then, completely involved with Bob. I hardly ever saw her, but we talked on the phone a lot. She used to talk to me about her job, but by this time it was all the problems of small farmers and the problems of the women that worked in the coffee. I could give a lecture on 'Women in Rural Jamaica' now, and I bet no one would know I hadn't done months of research on it.

Well, one day Katherine was going home in the car and she stopped in Gordon Town as usual and had a drink in one of the bars there. You know the one, Rocky's Hot Spot or something, with all this bamboo inside and old Joker Poker machines. Katherine had really got even more heavily into drinking since she had met Bob. She used to be able to drink beer, but by then, she could drink several shots of rum without feeling it. They'd gotten into the habit of regularly killing a bottle every time they opened one. She was in there, drinking enough rum to get her all the way home, when some man that she didn't know came and asked her for a lift. He said he lived at Violet Bank. She said no, because she didn't usually give men lifts, unless she knew them.

But when she went outside there were three women waiting beside the car with all their shopping, wanting a ride up the hill. By the time she'd loaded them all into the car, the man had come out of the bar and was asking for a lift again. With the other women there she felt safe, and there was room for one more, so she told him to get in.

Nothing happened until the last woman got out of the car at Plumtree, and then there was only the man in the car with Katherine. Plumtree is only about half a mile from where Katherine turned off the main road to go to the Porters' house, so she wasn't really worried. When she got to her turning she stopped to let the man out and he asked her where she was living, and if she lived alone. She didn't answer him, because of the threatening way he asked, and as she drove off up the road he called after her, 'I goin' come visit yu one of dese days.'

She was frightened and she told Louise about it when she got home. From the description of the man, Louise said it was probably the man they called Rat Man, who was just out of prison after serving six months for various thefts. Rat Man from Violet Bank. They had been expecting him back in the area for days. According to Louise, the man was a congenital thief. His parents despaired of him, and the last time, his father had taken a machete and run Rat Man out of the house into the hands of the police.

Louise reassured Katherine that Rat Man was not known to be violent, he was just a petty thief of such small account to anyone that the police in Mavis Bank would be happy to 'deal' with him if Katherine felt that he had threatened her in any way.

The police weren't very happy about having to spend time on petty thefts, when people were being murdered every day. But they had to in middle-class areas, because those people would always call the superintendent and complain that nothing was being done to recover their video recorders or whatever it was. So since the police were getting used to executing gunmen and murderers, to avoid all the trouble of going to court, they were beginning to carry out 'death sentences' on people like Rat Man who were no more than constant irritations.

Katherine just forgot about the incident. She felt safe, the man was known in the area as a thief, he was probably watched by everybody all the time. Although she objected to all the police executions going on, she was comforted by the thought that no one would knowingly risk their life for a few dollars of merchandise. Most of us thought that way then, although there was no evidence to support this view.

About three days after she had given Rat Man a lift, Katherine came home and Louise rushed out to tell her that someone had broken into the house through the dining room windows and stolen the radio and some jewellery. Louise had been doing the washing round the back behind her own house, and hadn't heard anything.

Katherine was very upset and went to report it to the police at Mavis Bank, who were not at all interested. They said they were sure it was Rat Man, it was exactly his style of operation, but he had probably already sold the things and so there would be no evidence. They were also a little contemptuous of Katherine, the way very macho men are of a woman who lives alone.

Bob was not that upset. It was the sort of thing he had expected to happen, what with Katherine having all and sundry in the house the whole time, and most of those people were very poor. He thought she was lucky to have gotten off so lightly, because after all, in Kingston in those days, they were driving up to houses with removal vans and taking every last piece of furniture and shooting the owners for good measure.

That Saturday Katherine made sure to tell everyone who came to the house about the robbery, and exactly what she'd lost, and how very upset she was about it. Bob just sat there and listened to her and didn't say anything, but she told me they quarrelled about it afterwards. He felt she was advertising her vulnerability, and she felt she was asking for help, the type of help that those people could easily give.

The next evening they were sitting on the verandah. It was after dark and Bob was just about to leave to go down the hill when they heard two vehicles coming up the driveway, and lots of people shouting. They heard, 'Miss Katherine! Miss Katherine! Come quick, ma'am!' Katherine told Bob to go into the house and watch from the windows, because they didn't know what was going on, and you know, he was a white man. Then she went around to the front, and almost ran back inside, because there were two pick-up trucks there, full of shouting men who were jumping to the ground. They were all carrying knives or ice-picks. Louise was standing there with her children. Katherine got a hold of herself, and went down the steps to stand by Louise. They were pulling a man out of the cab of one of the trucks. Rat Man. The men were shouting, 'We catch de t'ief! We catch him wid di tings dem.'

One of the men handed Katherine a crocus bag, which Louise grabbed from her, peered inside and announced triumphantly, 'Is Miss Katherine tings dem! See de radio. See de earrings dem!'

The men were now pushing and pulling Rat Man, who looked terrified and shrunken beneath his new flat cap, and the man they called Tinker, from Guava Ridge, was poking Rat Man in the ribs with the tip of his ice-pick.

'Miss, is this man t'ief yu things. Is what yu want us to do wid him?' one of the older men asked. He was holding Rat Man by the collar.

One of the other men said, 'We goin' kill him. We no keep any ras' t'ief in this district.'

'Miss, we catch him in the bush wid you tings. Is just for you to tell us what to do with him.'

But now the other men had taken up the call to kill Rat Man, and Louise was dancing around, shouting with them, 'Kill him. I want to see blood run in dis driveway tonight.'

Katherine was terrified. She and Rat Man. 'You can't kill him for stealing a radio,' she told them.

'But, ma'am is exactly dat him fe dead for. Yu want to wait, mek him dead for more than that?'

'You can't kill him over a radio.' Katherine was at least clear about that.

They were all disappointed at the prospect of being deprived of murder, except for the one other woman in the crowd, who said, 'She get her things back now. Mek we go.' The others ignored her, their eyes were fixed on Katherine. Decide.

Katherine wanted to appease the crowd, but also to show that they had to do this according to the law of the land. Whatever that was. Not according to the feelings of Tinker who was continuing to make casual jabs at Rat Man with the ice-pick. Rat Man was not even trying to keep away from the jabs. A dog would have been less resigned. The men were frightening, but she didn't want to follow her instinct to let them kill Rat Man and have done with it. What would she have done with his body, and what could she have said to the police? It was one thing for the police to execute people 'in hot pursuit' or to kill them 'returning fire' and another for a citizen to watch someone being slaughtered in her driveway. And Bob was in the house. He would not appreciate being a witness to a stabbing. Not when he and Katherine could identify nearly half of the men there.

'Can you please take him to the police in Mavis Bank? I reported the robbery to them. So if you could take him down there, and tell them that you caught him with the things, they could lock him up.'

The older man, Lloyd, immediately made a face, and said, 'We not taking him to no policeman.'

Louise, who had a natural sense of the moment, pointed a finger at Rat Man and shouted, 'I want a sacrifice. I want a sacrifice. Take off him clothes, I goin' burn them. He going home naked tonight.'

The men looked uneasy. Even Tinker stopped using the pick and stared at Louise. They didn't mind killing Rat Man but they weren't prepared to humiliate him in front of women. Not for being a thief. Katherine put what she meant to be a restraining hand on Louise, who shook it off. 'A sacrifice! A sacrifice!'

Someone pulled off Rat Man's cap and flung it on the verandah steps. They took off his belt and watch, and put them with the cap, and that was it, although Louise was evidently expecting more. She grabbed handfuls of the dry bamboo leaves that covered the driveway and flung them over the cap on the step. One of the men brought out some matches and lit the rubbish. The flames leapt up instantly and Louise threw more leaves on. It was quite a successful fire and Katherine saw the faces of the men relax as they watched it.

Tinker left Rat Man and came forward, 'Is a good watch. I want the watch.' He crouched down by the step and flicked the metal band of the watch out of the flames with his ice-pick, and then tried to pick it up with his hand, deliberately clowning. Everyone laughed as he dropped the watch and shouted in pain, and someone gave him a rag to pick it up with.

After that they all came and shook Katherine's hand and cuffed Rat Man around the head, as if he were a small boy, and in a few minutes they were back in the pick-ups, Rat Man in one of the cabs, squashed between two other men. They drove off, leaving Katherine staring in bewilderment at the smouldering fire, and then staring down the dark driveway. Louise threw some water from one of the garden barrels on the fire and shovelled the remains neatly off the steps.

'I see yu did frighten, ma'am,' Louise said. 'Is dat mek me mek the fire.' And that was all. Louise went off round to her own quarters, carrying the shovel full of smoking lumps of cap and belt.

Katherine took the bag and went back up on to the verandah. Bob was waiting for her with a large glass of ice and rum and lime.

'You were great! You handled that really well. Those guys are nuts. And Louise! I thought she was going to tear him apart with her bare hands, with all that Sacrifice, Sacrifice stuff.'

'She was just doing that as a diversion. So they wouldn't kill him.'

Bob liked Louise but he had never credited her with more than less-than-average intelligence. 'Well, she did a pretty good job of making out that she wanted to kill him too. All that shouting about blood in the driveway.'

'Well, I think she changed her mind. Anyway, I got my radio back, thanks to Tinker and friends. I'm sure Rat Man will think twice before breaking in here again.' Katherine felt vindicated. She had relied on the community and not on the police, and they had helped her.

'Maybe. Or maybe he's going to try and get even. You know, carry a grudge.' Bob did not mean anything by it, except that he was annoyed that Katherine was dismissing him as though he hadn't understood what he had just seen.

But he had really said the wrong thing. Because when Katherine was growing up, people carrying grudges had become dangerous. Really dangerous. She could remember the dozens of horrifying murders which the police would afterwards attribute to disgruntled employees, ex-partners, ex-husbands, old boyfriends, resentful sons. When Jamaican manhood had become synonymous with the frequent use of the penis, it also became synonymous with the frequent use of the gun. By then, almost anything could be the cause for murder. A harsh word to the gardener, five minutes too long talking to someone's girlfriend, bad driving . . . Every time it happened, within hours a thousand rumours would fly around town. Rumours designed to reassure. He was always cursing people, he was always hitting his workers, she was a real bitch, she never did anything for anybody. It won't happen to me, to you, to us, because we don't behave like that, nobody has any grudge against us . . . We were all happy to assassinate the reputations of the victims, even if we'd known them well, had never known them raise their voice to anybody.

It was definitely the wrong thing to say, and Bob was just trying to be right.But he got her where she lived, as the Americans say, and she got very angry. Told him to fuck off back to America, and stop hanging round her.

42

Bob left immediately. Went to work that next day, called me at nine o'clock in the morning and insisted on coming round to my office. He was cold. You could almost see the frost in his eyes. He called her 'Our cute dumb little friend'. Our cute dumb little friend is getting a bit out of her depth, and is taking it out on me.

I learnt how to be cold from Katherine. She was the world's expert in hardening of the heart. So when Bob was sitting there – thinking that because he was her friend, and over fifty years old, and a man, and a white man to boot, and he had suffered a grave injury to his self-esteem and to his heart, that someone, possibly me, was going to sympathise – I was trying to figure out some way to explain to him that it was the wrong approach and to the wrong person.

It wasn't that I didn't like him. I did. I liked Bob. He liked Jamaica, he preferred it to living in the States, and well, you know us island people – the ones that have gone away and come back – no matter how bad things get, we still defend Jamaica, we still feel that there's no better place to live, and no better people to live among. Someone like Bob comes along, old white American, and agrees with us, well, you almost have to like the man. Because, don't fool yourself, he didn't have an easy time of it in his business. There's no island paradise on Kingston wharf.

It was just that he had never come up against us when we feel an import is trying to make us behave. We're so proud, and so pleased that nobody, especially white people, can tell us what to do any more, that we get very unreasonable when someone like Bob starts thinking that there are certain standards of behaviour which he can apply to us, you know, just as if we were anybody. Certain standards like not hurting your friends.

It's a terrible thing, but here, we're proud of how unreasonable we can be. How dangerous we are. We think we're really dangerous. And we are. The men will kill you for any failure, at any time, to recognise what men they are, and the women will break your heart, just like that, and if that doesn't scare you, they'll tearfully confess that none of your children are yours, and that they've been sleeping with your father for the last ten years.

43

Down here, the women don't know the difference between one man and another.

Poor Bob. Even while he was telling me the story, I was getting angry. After all, why was he telling Katherine to watch out for Rat Man? Didn't she know the danger much better than he did? And why was he getting upset? He was very lucky to have met Katherine who didn't cost him much more than an occasional bottle of rum. He would have had to pay through the nose for any other woman. Especially since he was married. He was lucky that she had the stomach for his talk. Anybody else would have been demanding sex long ago, instead of having to be persuaded into it.

But I couldn't say that to Bob. He was miserable, miserable but confident that he was in the right. Which he probably was, but the only thing is, that there's no mediation any more. Dangerous people like to be recognised as such. They like to deal on their own terms.

We talked about it the whole morning, with everyone in my department getting curious about who I had locked in my office. Bob could talk, but all he kept talking about was how he was the kind of man who couldn't do this and couldn't do that. The main thing was that he couldn't understand how the friendship could have been lost because he threatened Katherine with Rat Man.

Katherine

The day after they brought back my things I didn't go to work. I knew Bob would ring me at my office, or try to see me. I also didn't feel like working. Rose was away in Trinidad and she was the only person I felt like talking to. By then, Rose and I had become good friends, although I didn't see her much except at work. Once Bob started coming to my office to take me out to lunch, she started paying more attention to me. Evidence of a social life, she said one day. Finally getting into having some fun.

I sat on the verandah in my sleeping shirt, watching the day. There were woodpeckers in the juniper trees on the lawn, but as the day got hotter they flew down into the forest. I could hear Louise moving around in the house. I could feel her wanting to talk to me, but I wasn't ready. I was full of pleasure at being home on a weekday, by myself.

Houses up here were built to be worked in and worked around. Just hearing Louise cleaning, and watching the gardener – Lloyd's cousin, Lawrence – wheeling compost from the heap down to the vegetable garden, made it a different place from the house where Bob and I drank rum and admired the view. Somewhere on the other hillside, out of sight, someone was clearing bush with a machete and you could hear every chop. An old man on a mule came ambling up on to the lawn out of the forest. The panniers on the back of the mule were full of carrots and skellion. He rode swiftly up to the verandah, jolting with the animal, one hand on the rope halter, the other tipping his hat. 'Ma'am. Morning, ma'am. Thomas, the name.'

The gardener had stopped and put down the wheelbarrow, but

started moving again once he saw me get up and lean over the verandah railings. Thomas looked as though he was still working on the old plantation, wearing khaki clothes and a battered hat.

Louise came out, looking embarrassed, and greeted him. He reached back into the panniers, and pulled out two sealed tins, which he tossed up to her. Even without the missing labels I recognised the distinctive product of the Blue Mountain coffee factory in Mavis Bank.

'Thomas' daughter work down the factory, ma'am,' Louise said, giving me a sideways look.

'You're going to market. The carrots look very nice,' I said to Thomas, who gave me a sweet, enthusiastic smile. He was almost toothless.

'Yes, ma'am. Best carrots from round Flamstead way. Mek me give you some.' He shifted the mule closer to the railings and gave Louise two handfuls of big fresh carrots. I was touched, as always. Bob laughed at how easily seduced I was by any kindness or generosity. It's as though you think there are no good guys left, he said. You think you're sitting in the camp and the cavalry has you surrounded.

I was thanking Thomas, and muttering to Louise, 'Do we have something to give him?'

'Thomas, you eat breakfast? You want saltfish fritter and green tea?' she asked.

Since Bob had been around, we had had plenty of saltfish. He could always get a few pounds and Louise and her children were visibly livelier on a Bob-supplied diet of saltfish for breakfast and plenty of fried and roast fresh fish for dinner. What I paid her had never come down to more than chicken-feed and cornmeal.

Thomas and Louise disappeared round to the side of the house for breakfast. It was still only about eight-thirty.

All morning I watched the traffic. Louise's friend from down the road, who came to drink tea. Two little boys wanting to pick the bitter Seville oranges that Mrs Porter had planted in a grove for her marmalades. A friend of Lawrence's bringing him bun and cheese and cigarettes. A small herd of goats and more small boys apparently taking the long way to the main road. A little girl begging flour from Louise. Two Jehovah Wickednesses, in a brown Peugeot, that Louise said had been trying to convert her for months. They came and asked me if I liked the view, and when I said 'Yes', they said, 'Wouldn't you like to look at it for Eternity?'

Is there anything one would want for Eternity? Just the thought was enough to make me want a cigarette. I had none in the house, and Lawrence had smoked his. I told Louise I was going to Plumtree for cigarettes, and she asked if she could come with me. She wanted soap and flour from the shop. We left the house in the care of Lawrence, but didn't bother to lock it up. After last night we felt invulnerable.

Driving down to Plumtree, Louise was careful to avoid mentioning Rat Man. She pointed out that the mango season was near, and that we would have a problem with all the children in the area, who over the last few years had been accustomed to take the fruit off the trees at the Porters'. I said, what problem? They could still take most of the fruit. Her own children and Lawrence would just have to be vigilant and make sure they picked the best mangoes for us. Most of the trees were far away from the house. We might hear the children but we wouldn't see them.

As we came round the corner before Plumtree, we saw a parked pick-up and two of the policemen from Mavis Bank, in plain clothes, and Roy, standing on the side of the road looking over the edge. I stopped without thinking. Any event warranted my attention up here nowadays, and I knew that Louise wouldn't want to miss anything involving the police. Neither did I.

'Yes, ma'am,' said the fat one, acknowledging my presence. Roy said hello to Louise but didn't look at me. About fifteen feet down the hillside, lying in the guinea grass, was the body of a man. There was blood on his shirt, and he looked like a dead animal to me. Crumpled, limp, unimportant. Like a dog hit by a car, that some pedestrian has pulled to the side of the road.

Louise said, 'Lord have mercy. Is dead, him dead?'

'Is Rat Man,' Roy said. I couldn't remember whether he had been up at the house last night. I didn't think so. Roy saying 'Is Rat Man' made me realise that the police had not killed him. They were here because there was a body, and when there was a body in

47

the grass below the road, the police were supposed to come. Louise had one hand pressed to her mouth.

The fat policeman said, 'I hear you have some trouble up your place last night, miss. I think they kill him when they carry him back down this way. They just kill him and throw him down in the bush.' He sounded disgusted. I wanted a cigarette.

Roy was watching me. We exchanged grave looks. The other policeman was apparently trying to find a way to get down the steep hillside to the body. Louise was shaking her head in distress. 'But is why dem kill him? You get your things back, and you tell dem they can't kill him.'

I started crying and the fat policeman glared at me for causing more problems. 'Well, ma'am, is not really your fault. These people up here, they wicked bad. Bes' thing now, is make yu drive me to Mavis Bank, and let me call one undertaker, and sen', call him mother and father.'

Louise and Roy wanted to stay. Louise was getting over it, and preparing to enjoy being first on the scene. She wanted to know how he had died. It was Roy who had seen the body and gone to call the police, although how he could have seen the body as he drove by was a mystery. You had to be standing right on the edge of the road, looking down, to spot it.

As I drove him to Mavis Bank, the fat man, Sergeant Williams, was also having doubts. 'Roy no see the man one ras'. Is tell him, somebody tell him and send him to look. Anyhow, we goin' catch dem ras'. You better tell me now who was up your place las' night.'

Why did he ask me that? How could I tell him who was there? Not Tinker from Guava Ridge, with his ice-pick. Tinker, who had recently built his own little shop at the crossroads, and who had helped push my car out of mud numerous times in the rainy season, in the time before I learned how to drive on mud. Tinker, who had two children and a girlfriend who worked in the coffee, and was always smiling and telling you jokes. Tinker, who hated a thief more than the devil because he made such a small profit on the cigarettes and beers and sweets he kept in his shop. Not Lloyd, who had spent his whole life working in the coffee, and now had a relatively good job as a driver, transporting the fertilisers and chemicals from Kingston around the estates. Lloyd, who couldn't persuade any of his daughters to go to school or to keep away from the men, and was faced with either throwing each girl out as she became pregnant by some indigent labourer or unemployed boy, or facing up to supporting dozens of grandchildren. Lloyd, who liked me for being single, and childless, and educated, and earning my own living.

The only men who had been there that I would have felt less guilty about implicating, were the unemployed ones; the ones that leant into my car and called me 'baby', wanted to know if they could come and visit me at night, the ones that lounged by the side of the road day and night waiting for something to happen, waiting for their girlfriends and babymothers to come home from work and cook for them. Who would miss them to a few years in the General Penitentiary? The women would just find other men to support. But none of those had been in the forefront of what happened last night. It was the 'serious' men like Lloyd and Tinker who'd been eager to punish Rat Man, who'd been pushing him around.

'I can't tell you that,' I said to the sergeant. 'Those people were just trying to help me. They caught Rat Man with my things and they brought him up to my place to give the things back. I can't tell you now who was there, so you can go and say they killed him.'

'Somebody kill him, ma'am. Somebody definitely kill him. And you're the same one that is going to come to the police next time somebody t'ief you out. I know you're a lady likes to live good with the people up here. But you don't know these people, ma'am. These same ones that come to your house to call Rat Man "t'ief", those same ones will come in your house tomorrow and t'ief you out same way.'

When we got to Mavis Bank, somehow the word had already gone around. Some people were looking at me with new respect, as if I'd ordered the killing. Or done it myself. I sat in the car while the sergeant went into the station. A few people came over to talk to me. We were all sorry to hear that Rat Man was dead. We all thought he was a bad, bad man. Still, God was merciful. God would take him up and wash him clean. Nobody seemed to think that there was a culprit. It was almost as if it had been an accident instead of murder.

After about half an hour the sergeant came back, told me I could go home. He was coming tomorrow to my house, but in the evening, to get a statement from me. Because you going to work tomorrow, ma'am, he reminded me. I'd forgotten this was Monday. What was I doing home in the middle of the morning on the first day of the week, except cleaning up after murder?

Louise wasn't back. I sat on the verandah and smoked cigarettes. Then I walked round the garden in the heat of the day with Lawrence, so he could show me what he'd been doing. There were lots of beans and callaloo and tomatoes in the vegetable beds, something had eaten all the lettuce. Elsewhere there were long rolling slopes of spiky, ragged grass with sprawling yellow raspberry bushes, wild sunflowers and guava trees. He had not been able to do much with ten acres of mountain garden. I realised he was going to need more direction, more seed, more fertiliser, less responsibility.

'Lawrence, you know what happened up here last night?'

'Oh yes, ma'am. I did hear dis' morning. I hear say dem kill him after they leave here. I hear say dem kill him.'

'Yes, well, you heard right.' I told him where I had just come from. He wanted to run down to Plumtree immediately, the thought of missing such an event was unbearable. I wanted to know if he had talked to Lloyd. Yes, he had talked to Lloyd. Lloyd had not been part of the killing. Lloyd was worried about what I would tell the police.

'But Lawrence, you've been here the whole morning and you never told me anything. When were you going to tell me?'

'Ma'am, I was going to tell you. But like how you never say anything to me, ma'am, I just wonder what you planning to do.'

For some reason I started shivering. You drove up here and the place looked almost empty. There were a few villages, mostly out of sight from the road, only a little shop or a bar, standing on a corner, to let you know there were people living in the area. You passed a few people on the road, farmers with machetes, children going to school, women waiting for a bus. But, otherwise, what did

50

you see? Forestry department plantations of Caribbean pine, bare, eroded hillsides patched with skellion, goats tethered on the verges, a few acres of flowers here and there, wynne grass, coffee, dirt roads that led nowhere, more blue mountains in the distance, mist. But the place was full of people. Full of people that knew every car, every jeep, every farm truck. People who knew that the Blue Mountain Angel lorry, which was coming from as far up as Hagley Gap, wouldn't come today. People who knew that the road had come down at Dublin Castle, twelve winding tortuous miles below. People that would wonder what the lady at the Porters' was planning to do about Rat Man in the guinea grass just above Plumtree.

'Well, Lawrence, you just tell Lloyd that I didn't know any of the people that came up here last night. I told everybody in the area that I got robbed. Some people caught Rat Man with my things. So they brought him up here. I didn't know the people, and it was too dark to see their faces properly. I told them to take him to the police, and as far as I know, that's where they were going when they left here. That's what I'm going to tell the police. I don't have any descriptions. The only person I ever saw before was Rat Man.'

I told him to take the rest of the day off – to go to Plumtree, to go to Guava Ridge, to go to Lloyd. I made it clear that I didn't want anyone coming to the house today to plead any case with me. I didn't want to discuss what had happened with anybody.

Lawrence left, but Louise didn't come. When her children came home I gave them peanut butter and crackers. They hadn't seen anything at Plumtree. There had been no one special on the road. They had got off the bus at our turning, as usual.

Louise didn't like the children to be alone in the house. The eldest girl was only ten. I sent her down the road to call Ruby, our neighbour, whose children were all big men now. When Ruby came I made her tea, gave her some rice and chicken to cook and told her to stay until Louise came. Ruby was aching to hear about last night. She had heard the pick-ups and the men on the road, but it was all over before she had managed to get out of bed and start up to the house. Her little field of yams and potato was on the

51

other side of the forest and she hadn't seen a soul all day except those ignorant Flamstead people who never knew anything. I left the children to give her their version. I was going to Kingston. To Carla, to rum.

I got to Kingston about six. The traffic was still heavy. Carla lived very inconveniently on the other side of town, in Red Hills. She had one of these huge five-bedroom concrete houses perched on a slope so sheer that the contractors had had to put in a three-hundred-foot retaining wall which cost more than the house. All her neighbours were similarly blessed, and after every earth tremor, they could be seen anxiously inspecting their property from the road for habitat-threatening cracks.

She was home. I parked on her concrete driveway and left the car in first gear – my handbrake not being equipped to deal with these gradients. Carla came to the door, naked under a large T-shirt, her breasts supporting 'Don't Mess With My Tutu', a bad taste souvenir of the Archbishop's visit.

'Hello, Worthless,' she said. 'You're really worthless. You didn't even go to work. I had your friend Bob crying in my office the whole day.'

'Well, just wait until you hear my worries now. Last night was the sweet part.'

Carla was a strict vodka drinker, but she kept a little dark rum for her friends. We sat on her verandah on fancy wrought-iron chairs, looking down on the flat Liguanea Plain, which used to be covered in sugar cane and was now covered in shanty towns, ghettos, no-go areas. Supposedly the legacy of slavery. And sugar. And bananas. We hadn't had mass tourism long enough for it to have left us with anything but dollars.

Carla asked lots of questions. As far as she was concerned the whole thing was just another episode in BMW, a documentary series aspiring to soap opera. Some entertainment value but not too much. That's why I wanted to see Rose. Rose had her own stories. Nothing was so bad that she could not distract you with her triangles, her weekends in Antigua with the consultant from

UNICEF, her disastrous room blocks at Pineapple Shout where the guests had to enter their rooms through breadfruit cascades.

'Bob,' Carla said eventually.

'Bob,' I replied.

Kingston was turning on its lights. Washington Boulevard curved its way to the fields of St Catherine. Out there things hadn't changed much. The Indian people in the sugar towns all had green 'puss eyes' nowadays, and they didn't remember how to speak Bengali or Hindi any more. They were more beautiful than their grandparents and they still cut cane.

'Bob's very upset about being told to fuck off back to America.'

You could rely on both Bob and Carla for exact quotes. Carla because she liked to be able to say, 'I'm TELLING you. It's a FACT.'

'So?'

'So, he's a friend of yours.'

'*Was* a friend of mine.'

'Bitch.'

'Thank you. Well, you can tell him to come up and see me at the weekend. I'll apologise.'

'Why don't you sleep with him?'

'He's married. He's supposed to sleep with his wife.'

'Tell me another one.'

'He's fat.'

'I think you should sleep with him. You've kept him hanging around long enough. You're not such great company. Also he's going back to America in two months' time.'

'News to me.'

'He was thinking of trying to stay longer. Talking to his partners about going into conch steaks.'

After I left Carla, I drove round to Poinciana Court. Sandy let me in, with a big smile. Carla didn't understand that that's why I didn't sleep with him. So I could go round to his house and say hello to his wife without feeling like a complete shit. How Sandy knew I didn't sleep with him, I don't know. Not because Bob told her. I was his fourth 'relationship' in five years, and he was an accomplished liar by this time.

Sandy said he had come in from work and gone to take a nap. I told her not to wake him. She offered me a drink, but she didn't have one. She just sat looking at me quietly, her soft American housewife hands folded in her lap. 'You guys had a quarrel?'

'Sort of.' I smiled at her. She looked away.

'Well, you know I'm the one that has to live with him. I haven't seen him this unhappy in years.' She was his keeper. The bear hasn't eaten this week and it's pacing its cage. Could it be allergic to captivity?

'Well, why are you worrying about it?' Why are you putting up with him? We were not friends, Sandy and I. She gave me a really nasty look.

'I'm his wife.'

'For all the good it does you?'

She laughed, forcing it out, her eyes hard. 'You wouldn't understand. He's a good man.'

'And you're certainly a good woman. The best. I don't know a lot of good women.'

She got up. 'Let me wake Bob.'

Bob came down, walked into the room like the master of the house, the way he never did in mine. To me, he always came diffident, uncertain, vulnerable, ten jokes rehearsed on the drive up the hill for my entertainment.

'Katherine.' I was amused by his coldness. The coldness of a man who doesn't know he can be cut out, cut off. From whatever it was I gave him, which had never been entirely clear.

'So how are you?' I said. 'Carla says you spent the whole day complaining about me in her office.' He thought Carla was his friend. He sat down, cold and getting colder.

'I think you were totally out of line last night. I think you were scared and just decided to take it out on me. I don't appreciate being bawled out like that, especially not by my friends.'

I told him about Roy finding Rat Man in the bush. He took the opportunity to let the quarrel drop. He was always generous like that. I think because he was close to being an old man. He didn't think it was worth it any more, pursuing injured feelings. Sandy had come back into the room in time to hear about Rat Man.

54

'You don't seem very concerned,' she said. Bob answered for us both.

'Well, there's not much Katherine can do now. The guy's dead. The main thing is to stop this whole thing from escalating.'

Sandy didn't say anything, just looked doubtful. I got up to go. Bob came out to my car with me, and leaned against the driver's door, arms folded, looking at me.

'So, Katherine, you haven't apologised. I thought we were friends.'

I looked around Poinciana Court, security lights, security guards, orange stucco roofs, fake ebony doors, birdcage verandahs, red Mercedes. What had I been doing with a 55-year-old white man from a place like this, if not sleeping with him? No wonder nobody believed we were friends. It was a joke, an impossibility.

'Sandy says you've been very unhappy.'

'Carla says. Sandy says. You could have figured it out yourself. If you cared at all.'

'Oh, I care. I was just thinking what a weird relationship we have.'

'It is weird. We should be lovers.' Bob could say that with his wife a few yards away in the house.

'What about Sandy?'

'I'm not offering to marry you, Katherine. I want to sleep with you, and I think you want to sleep with me. I'm accountable to Sandy, you're not. Sandy and I will figure it out.' He had so much confidence in his wife; or in his power.

'You're going to tell her? Hey, I'm fucking Katherine nowadays.'

Bob immediately started back towards the house – the discussion was over – and then stopped and turned to smile at me. 'You just go ahead and do what you want, OK? I hope everything works out over this Rat Man business. We're going back to the States in a couple of months and I'll come up to say goodbye before we go.' He went inside and closed the door.

I leaned against the car and tried to feel sorry enough for myself to cry. I repeated to myself what hurt the most – 'I'm not offering to marry you, Katherine,' and 'Sandy and I will figure it out.' It's not that I wanted to marry him, I wanted to be more than that. I wanted to be everything, indispensable. Much more than Sandy. Much more than any of his other girlfriends. Much more to him than anyone he'd ever known before, or would ever know. In return for which I would, of course, do nothing except continue to see him on the same basis as before.

I especially disliked Sandy for settling for so very much less, for willingly giving him up every weekend that year, for behaving as though I was a passing phase for Bob, for her assumption that she would always be married to him, and have the right to expect him home every day, no matter where he'd been or whom he'd been with. As though she was his mother, with dinner in the oven, and firm views on bedtime and homework. She was a temptation to me, I so wanted to prove her wrong.

At the same moment that I felt like going into the house and telling them both to fuck off, Bob came out again. He had a big confident grin, and a tie and a jacket.

'I'll take you out to dinner if you apologise.'

'Well, I don't think I'll be able to apologise on an empty stomach. You'll have to wait until after I've eaten.' I was as hostile as wanting to be loved permitted.

'You can say you're sorry in bed.' He took my hands and kissed them. How did he know I was ready to give in, give up, go to bed, make love? Maybe Sandy had just made some nasty comment about me, said something to let him know that I had offended her, finally – that we were prepared to fight over him now, so he could relax and stop worrying that we would both leave him at the same time, and for the same reason.

When Rose came back from Trinidad, Rat Man had been dead for a week. I didn't go to his funeral. Louise went, supposedly to represent me. I asked her how she had the nerve to go, when by this time everybody in the district, including his parents, knew about her calling for 'blood in the driveway' the night he was killed. Louise just laughed and said 'Is true, ma'am. Me mout' too big.'

The floor of Rose's office was covered with calypso and soca tapes and records which she had brought back with her. All the draughtsmen were in there, fighting over the most popular carnival songs, while Rose sat on her high chair ticking off names on a list and shouting prices.

'I want my money – oh! Don't let any of you come out of here with my good good music and don't give me my money.' She winked at me. 'This is not good business really. I can't make more than a few dollars on each tape.' Rose's mother had a shop in Port Antonio, and even when Rose was at architecture school in Chicago she had been expected to serve behind the counter when she was home on holiday. Rose told this story with pride and had never been known to go off the island for more than a day without returning with something to sell. Bob liked her for this. He was always shocked at the ease with which people cast off the source of their opportunity, when they scrambled, wallet first, into the middle classes.

Once she had disposed of most of the tapes Rose grabbed me by the arm and whisked me past the secretaries, muttering 'Lunch-time. Lunch-time.' It was eleven o'clock. 'I need a drink,' she said as we climbed into her gold Benz. 'I don't know why I bothered to come back. The place just depresses me. Where's Richard anyway?'

'Nobody's seen him since he went to Ocho Rios for the ground-breaking. He probably decided to make a long weekend of it.'

'Oh God. Welcome back to Jamaica. Richard's long weekends now last five days.' I noticed that she was heading downtown.

'Where are we going?'

'The beach. I didn't even catch sight of sea water the whole time I was in Trinidad. I want to eat some fish and festival.'

'Rose! No way! I've got a two o'clock meeting, and so have you.'

'Yes, but it's eleven o'clock. We'll come back in time.'

'I was supposed to be having lunch with Bob.'

'You're always having lunch with Bob. Have lunch with me today. When he comes to pick you up the secretaries will tell him

57

you went out with me and he'll figure out that you're not coming back for now.'

The beach was much too hot and windy for our office clothes. We sat inside one of the thatched huts where they cooked the fish, and drank cold beers. Rose listened to my robbery story, which had become almost funny by the fifth or sixth glib retelling. I told it as a picturesque piece about rural Jamaica, stressing the community spirit and all that. But Rose wasn't impressed and there was no way to make her laugh about Rat Man being murdered.

'You're lucky the police decided not to put the whole thing on you. Incitement or something. You see you! I can't believe you want to keep living up in a place like that where everybody knows your business and wants to interfere in it. It's dangerous.'

Rose, at forty-five, lived in a townhouse complex with her two children; and her privacy, and that of her boyfriend, and of the two married men she occasionally slept with, was a paramount concern. But, luckily for me, Rose doesn't like to dwell on uncomfortable topics. She lives in an area where there are four or five robberies per month and at least two murders a year. After establishing that the whole thing was my fault, she was content to leave it alone, and moved on to entertain me with a story about the New Building Materials conference she'd just attended.

Apparently someone had had the bright idea of inviting a delegation from Nigeria. The presence of six tall, stunning, Yoruba men, looking like every West Indian's idea of African kings in their flowing robes, had cut attendance at the seminars once they had indicated their willingness to fund elaborate parties at the poolside and in their suites. Women who had come to the conference as girlfriends, wives and secretaries, abandoned shopping expeditions to exhibit themselves in as little as possible, in the hope of getting what was quickly known as 'the real thing.'

Rose claimed that after one evening's partying one of the men had come out of his bedroom and sat next to her on the sofa where she'd been drinking his whisky for two hours. They talked architecture while he stroked her thighs. As people began to drift back to their own rooms, the Nigerian told Rose he would like to sleep with her. When she agreed instantly, he backed off, saying there was a girl still in his bed in the next room waiting for him, and she was unlikely to appreciate a request to leave. Rose was so annoyed, and so wet, she said, that she started hurling abuse at him, and to calm her down he suggested she should come to his room for breakfast a few hours later. Rose spent the rest of the night in her room wondering whether or not to go, but did in the end.

However, he was too exhausted to do much, and they'd ended up eating cold fried eggs in bed, while he cross-examined her about why she was not married. In Nigeria, he said, all women would do anything to marry and spent their lives either getting or trying to keep husbands. This had many social benefits, he maintained, as it gave men a proper sense of their own worth and inspired them to work and earn more money to support their wives and buy expensive presents for their girlfriends. That was another thing he didn't like, he said. In Nigeria, young and beautiful girls would not give the time of day to men without money, whereas these foolish West Indian women were opening their legs for nice smiles and nice lines.

At that point, Rose said, she had left hurriedly. She had just remembered it was time to call her boyfriend, who owed her twenty thousand dollars – he'd just bought a new car – and that she had promised to go to the campus and say hello to the daughter of one of her married men. She also had to go and borrow some money to give to the girl as her birthday present from her father, as he had been a bit short of cash and had not been able to send anything.

'Lord, child, the man was right. But you know what? I felt like going back in there and asking him for money. You know, say to him, "Look, since you understand how it is with us women here, how about giving me a couple hundred US dollars against my expenses?" ' Rose grinned at me.

'So did you?' She was certainly capable of it.

'No, I didn't have the nerve. But you know what? From now on I'm going to give Derek a hard time about the car money. Let him go and borrow money from the bank, and give me back mine. Let me get the interest on it, or at least I could use it to fix up the place on Stevens Road.'

Rose was looking irritated at the prospect of fighting with Derek, who would inevitably hug her and say, 'Of course, you're getting your money, baby' and then forget about it. The thought of Stevens Road cheered her up. She had three or four apartments around Kingston in semi-desirable areas, which brought her a steady stream of rent money. It was her main comfort, she said, every time she broke up with a man, and realised she was getting older and older, more and more likely to be spending her old age alone. She would review her investments and then go and sit with one or other of her contemporaries, who were married to rich men, and complained about the effrontery of their husband's latest girlfriend, and whether this affair was serious enough for them to wheedle six weeks in Europe out of him, or even a new car.

Her contemporaries, like the Nigerian, were alarmed at the increasing tendency of some young women, particularly the ones with good salaries, to adopt 'open leg policies' for very little financial gain. If their husband's girlfriends were not costing them an arm and a leg, it was unlikely that they would be willing to allow their wives to cost them the other arm and the other leg.

Rose and I were heavily under the Red Stripe by the time the fish arrived, and we were still laughing.

'So, how's Bob? How's the fish business? He should start selling Hellshire fried fish up there. Then he'd really make money,' Rose said, hands and mouth full of snapper, slices of onion slithering off the fish on to the table.

I wasn't sure if this was the moment to get the famous Rose perspective on Bob. I couldn't remember whether she even knew that I hadn't been sleeping with him all this time.

'He's all right. We had a few quarrels over this whole Rat Man business.'

'Oh, yes? Why?'

'Just over nothing.'

I suddenly realised that I didn't want to think about it. Nothing had changed really, except I had ended a long fast, a long friendship. It was the same thing – just more to like now, more to dislike later.

*

I used to have a friend, when I went to school in England. He was a portrait painter, and my mother sent me to him to have my picture done. He didn't ever paint me; first because he was too busy, and then because he was too ill. We were only friends for the last four years of his life, and he was nearly sixty when I met him.

In the last thirteen or fourteen years whenever I tell a story, or think of telling a story, I'm always telling it to Santo. He was half Spanish and so good looking that women deliberately looked away when he came into the room, tried to ignore him. I went to visit him late in the evening, when he would be sitting alone and very sombre in his living room.

He liked me to come and talk about school, and my friends and all the concerns of a sixteen-year-old girl, none of which had ever been his concerns. He had always been loved, always been different, always been special. He had not been poor, except as a child; he had lived his whole life between a small town in Spain and a small town in England, and what with love, and work, and money, he had made himself content.

Santo. I still wake in the night and cry because he's dead. He was the only person I knew who took the trouble to explain himself properly. That's what I had a yearning for, to know everything.

He knew that I loved him, and he never pretended to think of me as a daughter or anything like that. I don't think he had ever known a woman that didn't love him, or wasn't prepared to love him. He treated me like a woman, and he never made love to me because, by then, he felt too old to make love to all the women that wanted him, and I was the least eligible – by age and inexperience. He lived alone because his wife had died.

People said that he made a strict rule of only sleeping with women in his studio, and he was home every night by seven. He always took his wife with him to Spain, and in Spain as well he only slept with women in his studio, and he was home every night

61

by six, because there he used to go for a walk with his wife every evening. He never had affairs, and he was married for thirty-six years, and no woman ever interfered with his wife.

He didn't marry again when she died because he said that if he couldn't be with her any more, he was better alone. He kept to the old habit of refusing to have affairs, and although he continued to sleep with women in his studio, he would never have them in the house. He let me come to the house, because he didn't sleep with me. I was privileged. When I heard he was the best lover in the world, I wasn't tempted. He never slept with any woman more than three times. That was because, he said, after that, sex interfered with his work and the women began to expect things.

He never had any problem with women, but he was disliked by most men. He rarely met a man who didn't have a wife or a girlfriend, a sister or a mother – and the women always very obviously wanted to sleep with Santo, and Santo rarely turned down a woman on the grounds of age or appearance or martital status.

He lived as if he accepted the mores of his neighbours but had simply failed to understand exactly what these were. They called him 'That man', or, in the case of the women, 'Oh, that man!' When I asked him if his wife had ever had affairs, he said he had never asked her.

'Don't try to know everything about someone you want to live with all your life. My wife knew that I slept with other women, but not because I ever told her. Just because women don't keep quiet about such things. Other people told her. But I never gave her any evidence of it. I was always home when I wasn't working. I spent regular hours in my studio. I never went to London or Spain or anywhere without her. If she couldn't go for any reason, then I didn't go either. I was the most uxorious husband in the world. If my wife ever wanted to come to my studio she telephoned me first, and I made sure she never came upon anything there.

'I never kept a bed in the studio. I always make love on that big table at the end of the room, or on the floor. When you do it like that, most women don't feel comfortable talking afterwards. You put on your clothes, they put on their clothes. Then I walk over and kiss them goodbye, and they know they should leave. If I'm painting them, I don't let them stay after we've made love. They have to leave and come back the next day. And because women talk, after a very few years, almost all of them knew what to expect. I was married, I never slept with anyone more than three times, if that. I would never see them outside the studio, I never entertained any conversation or discussion about relationships, or about my wife. They can tell me what they like. I think I'm probably the nicest thing that ever happened to most of them. They knew exactly what they were getting from me, and that's all most of them want. Certainty about a man. Do you see?

'My wife taught me that. She may have had lovers, but she would never have left me because she knew I would never leave her, and I was the best husband in the world for her. We kept silence on that one thing only. Like a secret between us. And because of that thing that I had, because I had that place to be alone, to do only what I wanted, I never felt like hurting her or being away from her. And it was the same for her.

'Imagine, Katherine, how it is to be with a man who leaves you entirely to yourself every day. Time when you can do whatever you want to, without asking permission, without having to give any account of your activities except if you want to give one. But you have to do something with your time, it can't be time spent waiting.

'My wife was completely special in that respect. She never waited for me. She had the children and she read, and she thought, and she worked at all kinds of jobs, and if she was ever idle, she never mentioned it to me.

'But because of our secret I often came home, a little bit alert, a little bit aware, in case something or someone had happened that would have made her change her mind about our secret. And I think that she sometimes noticed if I was very tired or very absent-minded when I came home, and maybe she wondered, has he met the one that he will leave me for? Although we were very married and very close, it was always a little bit like watching someone from a window when they don't know you're there. You know how that is? When they do something that they only do because they think they're alone. I used to watch her for signs like that – signs of how it was for her when she was alone. And of course the watcher is always alone in the window, alone and silent and aware.'

Santo. He told me that if I couldn't find a man like him, I should never marry. It was a weary thing to say to a young girl. I told him. He said, 'Some people don't like to be left alone. They are so little to themselves, bad in themselves, weak, bored, tired of life, so corrupt they can't support their own company. They have to be reassured, distracted, diverted, enhanced, reduced – anything not to be themselves. You see, some people are without resources, and it's best to keep yourself from such people. They will just want your resources to keep them from themselves. If you marry a man like that, you can never be alone. He will try to put himself in your mind, use you up, tire you out, make you wait for him. You will never be alone again, you will never watch from the window, because you'll always be down in the street trying to stop him from being alone, and trying to stop yourself from seeing him, how he is when he's alone. Because it will be something unbearable. It is bound to be.

'You see I loved my wife for herself, how she was when she was not with me. And she loved me because all she wanted from me was that I should be a man who would always love her and never leave her. And that's what I was, even when I was alone in the studio, I was still the man who was coming home to her. Even when I made love to other women, I was still the man that would always love her and never leave her. And we were all right together, do you see? She was so alone. She had me, she had everything, and she was most happy when I was at the studio and she knew I was coming home to love her, but I wasn't there right then, being with her. She only wondered about me when I was there. Do you see?'

Santo. I always talked to him. After my father met him, and didn't like him, my father mocked, 'Do you see? Do you see, dearly beloved? I hope you don't believe all his fairy stories.'

I believed him implicitly. He said I could be alone, not without love, but without the kind of trouble that not being alone can bring on a person. The kind of losing yourself, the part that could be alone, and let other people alone. I used to talk to him. Santo, you say you loved your wife, but you think hell is other people. You say your wife loved you, but she was only really happy when you weren't there.

He would laugh, he had such a mouth, such heavy, dark, sweet lips, and deep white teeth, that when he laughed I would get caught up in his mouth and forget what we were laughing about. And when he was listening he looked serious, sombre, grave, and his dark eyes were kind, tender, loving, listening. He was kind to me, with my endless stories about my teachers, my school, my friends, the boys I liked. He knew that I told him about those boys to make him jealous, and he was happy to play that game with me. He would ask me lots of questions about the boys, as if it mattered to him, and would always look grave and conclude, 'He's not good enough for you.' I loved that. I loved talking to him. Talking to him was a delight. He could paint a portrait and then give you ten thousand words about it. He could tell me more than I was ever capable of seeing.

I asked him how he could sleep with so many women, and he said he liked making love and he liked women. He said it was a way of being alone. He said he couldn't be alone with his wife, because when he was with her, he wanted to be with her. I asked him how he could sleep with all those women, and not have any relationships. It was so unfair. He said they always knew what they were getting, and they could always decide. He said he knew how to make love properly, to please himself and to please a woman. Every woman got that from him. If he didn't think he could make love to a woman properly, because of something about her, or because of the way he was at the time, he wouldn't make love to her. He said he made love to women, and gave them a place to be alone. Something nice happened to them, and it was only for them.

I asked him why he had got married if he wanted to be alone so much. He said he didn't know how to be alone unless he was with someone most of the time. He said he needed to love, and it was very difficult to find a woman that he could really love. When he met his wife and fell in love with her, he made up his mind to

65

marry her and always to love her, and that she would be the person he would be with. And so he stopped himself from ever being with anyone else.

I asked him about his children and he said they were fine, but they mostly left him alone, because when their mother died they found they didn't know him, and he was too old now, to let himself be known.

I said, 'But you let me know you.' He laughed and said, 'You are your own answer.' When I complained that he never really explained things to me, he never satisfied my need to know how things were with him, he looked grave. He said I had to learn how to leave people alone. He was his own answer, and if that didn't satisfy me, nothing would. I would become one of those women that he had always avoided – the ones that would not take what they were given, but go around the side entrance and devour the giver.

'I give you so much, Katherine,' he said, and he said it as if he were pleading. 'You don't know what I give you. But you will find it out.'

I have found it out, Santo. I have found it out, and Bob has found it out in me.

*

At first, when I met Bob, I almost forgot about Santo for a while. I thought Bob was him. Sitting around and talking, and just enjoying being together, I thought it was the same thing. I didn't realise that Bob could sleep with me and turn me into a woman who didn't want to be left alone.

Once we were sleeping together, I became very conscious of sex. It stopped bothering me that the people in my office were constantly having affairs, mostly with each other. But I noticed more how people were getting hurt. I could get hurt the way Suzette had been hurt, or the way Rose was hurt, or the way Judith was hurt. Rose was usually my source of information because Rose could make anything palatable, and everyone told her their business. It was her experience that the devil took the hindmost, and purgatory took the rest. 'I'm in purgatory,' she would come moaning into my office, 'but at least there's still a chance of working my way up.'

She was in purgatory because she was insisting on recovering her twenty thousand dollars from Derek, and Derek was considering leaving her to avoid paying the money. Richard thought she was unreasonable.

'Forty-five-year-old men have to pay all kinds of wages to have a relationship. What makes you think you can get off scot-free? Leave the man with his car.'

'Oh yes.' Rose was indignant. 'I didn't see you turning over any cash to Suzette when you were screwing her.' Richard winced at the 'screwing'. He didn't like bad language in mixed company, but he couldn't avoid it when he was mixing with Rose.

'That's different,' he boasted, 'I'm the boss. The boss doesn't pay his secretary for that. She takes it as a bonus.'

'He took her to California,' I pointed out. 'You think Suzette was getting to California any other way? He doesn't pay her enough.'

'Yeah, I took her to California.' Richard was pleased with himself for having actually done something for Suzette and wandered off. Rose just looked at me and made a face.

'Now he thinks he's great. Anyway, that's her problem. My problem is what happens to my money if Derek leaves me?'

That's what I asked Bob. What happens to Rose's money if Derek leaves her? He smiled. It was Saturday afternoon, at my house.

'Well, what did she do? Take the money out of her savings account and give it to him?'

'Yes.'

'Well, it's gone. She just believed he was going to pay it back, and he probably isn't going to. Tough.'

'That's it? Tough? She can't do anything?'

Bob shrugged. 'She should have got him to sign a promissory note or something. She can't prove she gave him the money on the understanding that he had to pay it back.'

'Of course she didn't ask him to sign anything.'

Bob looked cynical. 'So now she's out of twenty thousand bucks. Rose knows the score. Anyway, how come she's out of love so fast? I thought she was crazy about him. Isn't that the one that gets up and makes her breakfast every Sunday morning?'

'Yes, but she met this Nigerian who told her that men have to pay for it. Told her she was dumb to have been giving it away free. He reckoned that women giving it away free was damaging to the social fabric. If men can fuck for free, they won't work.'

Bob put back his head and laughed in an embarrassed way, as if I'd caught him out. 'Where'd she meet this guy? In bed?'

'Yes.'

'Well, she should know better than to believe what a man tells her in bed.'

'I'll remember that.' And I did, although it didn't stop me from remembering every single thing he said to me while we were making love, so that I could repeat it back to Rose at work. Carla didn't like to talk about these kinds of things, but Rose loved it.

'I like it when they're crude,' she told me. But sometimes when I was telling her, although she laughed, she looked a bit sad for me, as if she knew that telling all was a bad sign. I knew it was a bad sign. That's why I did it.

I was building my raft in case I was going down river.

Carla

Katherine said that sleeping with Bob didn't change anything, but, as far as I was concerned, it changed a lot. It was embarrassing to be a third person when Katherine was with Bob. She couldn't keep her hands off him. It would really upset me to go to lunch with them and be sitting in some expensive restaurant full of people while Katherine pawed at this old, fat, white man. It was completely undignified. Bob liked it. He would just smile and shrug, and look at her fondly, as though he sympathised with her for being in love. It was so embarrassing that men who were sleeping around the day after their wedding, like her boss, Richard, spoke to her about it. I knew what they meant, but I felt for Katherine.

Fucking around was supposed to be about sex, and about getting something just for being older and being younger. You know how we are. If you're a young single girl you're supposed to look sexy and expensive and well worth the money, and if you're a married man you're supposed to look smug. You know – like how they look at the traffic lights when they're sitting in their new BMW Sports, and everybody's looking to see what model it is. All this love business, as her boss put it, was a joke. It looked to the men as if Bob was setting a bad example by getting something for nothing – because Katherine looked nice but inexpensive – and it looked to the women like Katherine had a man that really cared for her. It only upset people. The whole thing seemed to lack caution.

Katherine told me that Louise even spoke to her about it. Louise changed the sheets and she knew the time when Katherine stopped keeping Bob as a friend and started keeping him as her man. Came and told her, 'Ma'am, he can't marry you, why you troubling yourself about the man?' Because Louise thought that one of the benefits of being a middle-class woman was that you could get married. It was only poor women like her that had to take their men and their children on the street, and she objected to Katherine behaving like one of the girls from Guava Ridge. How could Katherine expect any of the women around the place to respect her when she was acting like she didn't have any background?

Katherine's answer to everything was 'Leave me to enjoy myself. I'm in love.' That also upset people. She went through a few weeks of trying to detach herself from Bob, at least in her mind. Then she gave up, and decided she was as happy as could be. When Louise said to her, 'He's married,' she said, 'I know.' When I asked her, 'What about Sandy?' she replied, 'What about her?'

I never would have thought it would turn out the way it did. Katherine was so calm and cool before she was sleeping with him, there didn't seem to be anything wrong with her sleeping with him. That's why I encouraged it. I thought she could handle it, and anything else seemed less than what Bob deserved.

Bob was such a nice man, although he had this habit of telling you what he thought. He liked me but he didn't like my story. He even liked my brother, but he didn't like the fact that I was in planning and that my brother was one of the three biggest developers on the island.

'You don't talk to him about your work?' he asked me one lunch-time. Katherine nearly suffocated trying not to laugh when I said, 'Of course not.'

That's how nice Bob was. You couldn't say to him, 'Look, fool, look where I live. You think I make that kind of money?' No, I told him that my brother had built me the house as a present. A little present for helping to take care of the family, and taking care of the family was very important. Just taking care of ourselves wouldn't have made me a resident of Red Hills, or my brother one of the three top developers in the island.

Bob, as I realised after a while, had a blind spot about business interests that weren't his. When he was talking about BMW he couldn't understand the poverty wages that were being paid in the coffee, when Blue Mountain coffee couldn't be had for love or money except if you were Japanese; or why Forest Industries could make the men up there haul logs in the middle of the night and then only pay them two months later, and pay them only half of what was due, when you couldn't get hold of enough wood to build a garden shed. He spent lots of time on the phone abusing the local capitalists on behalf of the local poor. He had this idea that people were making a lot of money and they weren't spreading it around.

Rose, Katherine's friend at work, pointed out that while Bob had this nice sociable line in fresh fish and saltfish for all his friends, all his money was regularly converted into US dollars and repatriated to his account with First Fidelity. If you ever needed to do any dealings on the black market Bob was your man. He could change you a hundred dollars, and he would turn out to be the personal friend of the guy that could change you a hundred thousand. Some of the nasty rumours that always circulated about any foreign businessman in Kingston were very nasty rumours when they were about Bob. Supposedly, Bob was just like that with a number of major ganja smugglers, and the US Drug Enforcement Administration was just like that with Bob. He was supposed to be the broker who decided who went to prison and who would be found decomposing off the road to Port Royal.

Katherine said, Yes, and he only does all this stuff for BMW because he's secretly working for the CIA.

Richard was fond of Katherine because she came across as so wide-eyed, such a fool. Richard was much too far gone to care about anyone that looked as if they could take care of themselves. Richard said Bob was not the sort of man to be trusted.

'You can't trust anyone,' Katherine said, 'and he's no less trustworthy than anyone else. I'm not trustworthy. I'm only in love.' Richard told her to come and boast about it when Bob and Sandy were holding hands back in the States.

People that didn't like Bob said he was a hypocrite, and Katherine said he was full of contradictions. Of course that's why she loved him. He was so various.

Katherine

After Rat Man was killed, and the police didn't arrest anyone for it, it appeared that almost everyone between Gordon Town and Guava Ridge had been up at the Porters' house that night. It appeared that I owed a great deal to a great many. Bob told me to refuse to consider whether or not I was under any obligation. Just make it clear that anything you do for people is because you want to do it, not because you owe it to them. But maybe I owed it to them?

If you do, Bob said, you'd better figure out what it was worth to you, and how you're going to pay it back. Maybe you can organise a death squad against some of the other petty thieves around here. Starting with your friend, Lloyd.

Lloyd had recently been fired supposedly because of the inordinate number of sacks of fertiliser that went missing from his truck between the farm store in Kingston and the farm. He had come to see us and explained that some of his neighbours grew coffee, and they didn't like it if Lloyd couldn't 'free up' a few sacks of fertiliser now and again. He said the real reason he'd been fired was that the foreman's brother was a driver, who had just returned from a job in St Mary. The brother got Lloyd's job. Within two weeks my friend Lloyd who used to stop his truck when he saw me on the road and joke with me for five minutes about his troublesome daughters and all the worthless people he had to work with, was waving me down to tell me he had no food in the house, the babies were hungry et cetera. He was bitter enough to take money from Bob. I never offered him any, against the day when he would be working again and we could meet as friends.

Bob said you can't afford to have friends that are so much poorer than you are. There's no way to avoid being their benefactor. Lloyd needs benefactors, he can be friends with Louise who at least can appreciate his worries. You, all you can do is be appalled.

I had to stop being appalled shortly after Rat Man got killed. I stopped having enough time to be horrified by anything. BMW's resources, in the form of Bob and I, were stretched to the limit in an effort to prevent us from killing each other, getting married, breaking up, running away together. On the days on which I called him at his office to tell him I loved him and couldn't we move to one of the other islands where he could go fishing and I could build houses, Bob had to say he liked it right here in Jamaica and he was sure I'd be miserable without Richard and Rose and Carla. On the days when he came rushing up to the Porters' saying he was going to ask Sandy for a divorce and carry me off to the Bahamas, I had to say I didn't want to marry him and the only place I hated more than Nassau was Miami. That was easy.

It was when he told me that I had to learn how to stop being such a soft touch, because I'd given two dollars to a little boy cleaning windscreens at the traffic lights – the same little boy to whom Bob normally gave five dollars for the same inadequate smearing around of the Porters' driveway mud – that was when it was hard. When I told him I was sick of him drinking half a bottle of rum on Saturday, and half a bottle of whisky on Sunday, even though he never got drunk, I could see him deep breathing so as not to hit me. That was the other thing – although he was very gentle, he was also a hitting sort of man. He would talk, talk, talk, drink, talk some more, but I could tell it was just a way of not hitting me.

Carla said, As long as he never hits you. Everybody feels violent sometimes. But Bob felt violent a lot of the time. He loved me but I frustrated him. He saw things simply; I was sure everything was much more complicated than it looked. When we were talking about Rose, I saw a woman who had fashioned her life, and had made a success of it; Bob thought she was a disappointed woman who was good at making the best of things. Most importantly, Bob thought he was entitled to his opinion and I was never sure that he was.

Bob thought we had to make a few compromises. I realised he was trying to bully me into submission. When we agreed to disagree, he would get annoyed when I made one last attempt to make him see it my way. Bob thought our relationship was about being in love, talking, going to the beach, making plans, going to bed. I wanted him to tell me things that I didn't know already.

'How can I? You think you know everything already.'

'No, I don't.'

'Yes, you do.'

He could remember every single time I'd ever contradicted him. Before we were sleeping together I responded very well to Bob's monologues. I would ask questions about details, laugh at the jokes, lead him into the next story. By the time we were sleeping together we were nearly getting to discussing his marriage to Sandy, his second wife. I didn't want to hear about the marriage to Sandy. As I loved her husband more and more, I felt more and more guilty about Sandy. I could feel how she must love him, not want to lose him, and I knew as well as she did how very willing he was to lose her.

Bob was like me. He preferred to be the only witness to what he'd done and been. Other people's memories of the same events only spoiled our stories. They didn't remember us as we knew we had been then. Sandy was there when Bob was struggling to build a business, I was told about the inevitable triumph. I knew the man who had been bound to succeed. And Bob knew Katherine as presented by Katherine. He never challenged my version of events, and I never challenged his.

At first, of course, when I thought he was Santo Mach II, I thought this was because we knew how to leave each other alone. Once I slept with him, loved him, I started worrying that it was because he didn't care enough to notice that I was slightly imperfect. I started criticising him as I hadn't done since the day we went on the boat. I remembered why we had quarrelled the night Rat Man was killed. I realised I had been massively duped into believing that Bob was a kind, gentle, reflective, interesting,

75

understanding man – unlike all other men. He told me all those things about himself and I'd accepted him, and them, without doing any primary research.

Primary research revealed he was opportunistic – business, manipulative – women, selfish – Sandy, unkind – Sandy, patronising – me, overbearing – me, a terrible liar – rumour, a crook – rumour. When I confronted him with this evidence of duplicity, he laughed and hugged me, and said, 'I used to think you were pretty nice too.'

Rose encouraged me enthusiastically to love Bob. She was back in love with Derek who'd been promoted and had a company car. He sold his new car, extorting twice what he'd paid for it from someone who couldn't get an import licence, and gave Rose back her twenty thousand dollars, having cleared a hundred thousand on the deal. Rose had really wanted to ask Derek for some sort of commission, or interest, on her money, which he'd had for over a year. Richard told her it was time to get back to the real world.

In the real world Bob was negotiating with his partners for more time in Jamaica. I never gave it a thought. We were building a spa on a sheer rock face in Portland and I was out of Kingston three days in the week. Then the roads collapsed at one of the new coffee plantations in the Yallahs Valley and, although it was a long way into the mountains from where I lived, the worries of the fifty or sixty people thrown out of work began filtering back to BMW. Lloyd had disappeared, apparently to look for work in another part of the island. His daughters were pestering me for jobs cleaning, sewing, cooking, looking after children, as none of their babyfathers were in a position to contract for these services. Their own children began appearing on the road looking for mangoes, three- and four-year-olds that looked and smelled motherless.

I was always busy and always tired. On weekends I started getting up at five o'clock in the morning to have time to go walking by myself. When Bob came we often spent whole afternoons in bed, not making love but sleeping. I only slept well when he was there. By myself, during the week, I stayed up late reading and smoking, trying to think, trying not to come to any conclusions. A few times Louise came and knocked on the verandah door and told me to go to bed.

One night I came back early from Portland where we'd discovered the Caribbean Sea running deep and blue under the rock where we were planning to put the foundations. Someone, not me, was going to have to mention it to the client. For the first time in a long time I was home before sunset and drank a whole jug of rum and orange juice on the verandah. I was asleep on the sofa, which I had dragged outside, when Bob came. He spent about five minutes telling me how crazy I was to go to sleep with the house open, and no one around to make sure I didn't get my throat cut. Then he made another jug of rum and juice and got on to the sofa with me.

'I have to go to the States tomorrow. To see my partners.'

'How long for?' He often went back for a few days, on business. To count the takings at First Fidelity, Rose claimed.

'A couple of weeks. We've got to think up a whole new distribution system for the gourmet side. I'm taking Sandy with me.'

'Are you coming back?'

He looked at me, held my hand. 'Of course, I'm coming back. What's the matter?'

'Just that if you're not coming back, you should tell me. You know, so I can look for another fish supplier.'

He was supposed to laugh but he didn't. He let go of my hand. 'You can go downtown at seven o'clock in the morning like everyone else. See what's come in.'

'But you are coming back?' I said seeking reassurance.

'I have to. I'm not tired of you yet.'

'Good. Guess what happened today on site.'

'You found the sea. I called your office to find out if you were back. Rose says she's spending the night moving all the buildings half an inch to the right. She wanted to know where the hell you were.'

I laughed. 'She's going to have to move them much more than half an inch. There's probably sea all the way up under the main complex.'

'Well, isn't that why you should be down there? Helping them figure it out?'

'The client had the site surveyed, Bob. He had a geologist, he had loads of consultants. They didn't mention the sea. I think that if they missed that much water they might have missed a few other pertinent facts.'

Bob got up and leaned on the railings. He was tired, upset about something more than going to the States tomorrow. I waited for him to talk about it. Without turning, looking out to the mountains it was much too dark to see, he said, 'Katherine, Sandy wants me to stop seeing you.'

War. Eleven months into negotiations for partition. I didn't say anything, just caressed my calves, hugged my knees, made sure I was still all there, warm, soft, capable of inspiring emotion, love, devotion.

'She says she's had enough. She says I'm just trying to stay in Jamaica because of you. She wants us to go back to the States.' Still giving me his back, round shoulders with a long scar on the left one from an accident in a car. In a bar. He was fifty-five and he drank too much – was still known to get into fights in bars. A nice man, a hitting sort of man. He cried sometimes; to be alone, close to death, in love, helpless, too powerful. He often didn't know what to do with himself. Like Santo, when I knew him – wise and futile.

I went, put my arms around him, buried my head in his shoulder, stroked the back of his head. We went inside to make love; that night it was enough to calm us both. We had that, and it was sweeter than ever.

The two weeks they were in America I panicked. I went to stay with Carla. She suggested it, after Rose called her and told her she'd found me crying in my office. Rose knew I couldn't go and stay with her, in her life of perpetual, enjoyable complications. Rose thought, That's the way things are. You'll love again. It's a learning experience. He'll leave his wife. Don't worry. Everything will work out all right.

Carla cooked for me every night, bought cartons of cigarettes, bottles of rum, told me to shut up and eat, shut up and smoke, shut up and drink, shut up and sleep. Carla didn't recognise that I had a problem. Bob had gone to the States with his wife for two weeks. Big deal. His wife wanted him to end the relationship with me. What did I think she was? An idiot? A saint? She'd been wonderful considering the disgraceful way her husband had behaved up until now. Not many Jamaican women would have put up with it. Did I think Bob was just going to stay in Jamaica year after year, living with Sandy and visiting me? Just like that, no problem?

I don't know what I thought. I thought there was no necessity for me to think about anything. The kind of things that I might have had to think about I had taken care of – I had a job, life insurance, I lived in the mountains, I lived alone. Those were fundamentals. Bob didn't change any of those things. They were not the question.

'Well, if Bob hasn't changed anything, why are you so upset? He'll leave you. No problem.'

I was just as upset at the prospect of him leaving Sandy and moving in with me, or worse, expecting me to move to Washington with him. Not that I didn't love him, wouldn't have moved anywhere to be with him. Just that I didn't like the way Bob lived with Sandy, and I had a suspicion that that was the way he would live with me. Once I knew him well enough for him to feel that I didn't know him at all.

He telephoned me at the office every day. His partners thought it was OK if he wanted to spend another year in the Caribbean, but he was depressed about being in Washington, and seeing all his old friends. He'd forgotten how much he missed sailing on the Chesapeake. Sandy was having a wonderful time, shopping and visiting. He hadn't told her yet that he had decided to spend antoher year in Jamaica and she was going to be very upset.

I suggested that Sandy spend the next year in the States and he could go up one weekend a month to see her. It would give us time to figure out what to do. Bob didn't think that was such a good plan because Sandy wasn't used to being on her own. Carla laughed at the very idea. 'He's not used to being on *his* own! The way things have been, she's the one that's been keeping her own company.'

After a few days in Red Hills with Carla I was suffering from an overdose of good company and good food. On the third day I was dreading going to her house after work because Carla's friends congregated there for one or two hours every evening. Most of them were involved in politics in some way, and since we were just beginning to feel the pain of the latest IMF agreement, the conversation rarely varied from policy options, panaceas, past, present and future prime ministers. Although Carla had no problem switching from a heated discussion about the vital necessity of weaning the masses off saltfish while maintaining a steady supply of incentive 'Oh Henry' candy bars for the middle classes, to the heartaches of Katherine, it embarrassed me. Relieved to drop the divisive issues they had probably been discussing since the newspaper landed on their lawns at 7.0 a.m., her friends all started giving me examples from their own lives, followed swiftly by the kind of 'almost-failsafe' advice we got from the IMF.

I was told the most terrible stories. One of the women had married her lover, after she had encouraged him to divorce his wife. When she protested about his new girlfriend, he told her that his previous wife had never complained – she was the trouble-maker.

One of the men had been followed to his girlfriend's house by his wife. When he left, his wife had gone to the house and stabbed the girl in the shoulder when she opened the door. He had nearly ruined himself trying to keep the whole thing quiet, then his girlfriend took his wife to court for grievous bodily harm, his wife had sued him for divorce on the grounds of mental cruelty, and he had ended up with the last two 'male responsibility' judges in the legal system, and been forced to pay costs for both the women, in addition to a crippling settlement. His wife had come out of prison after three months and fled to America with the children. He had no idea where she was, and he hadn't seen his children in four years.

Another woman had lost her job and been disowned by her

managing director boyfriend after she became pregnant and refused to have an abortion.

The basic message was heads you lose, tails you lose. When you win, you wished you had tried for something or someone else. Purgatory, as Rose would say. I hugged Carla, and thanked her for raising my level of conscious fear. Before staying with her I had only been afraid of rejection and commitment, now I was also afraid of betrayal, ridicule, assault, pregnancy, exposure. Carla said she always tried to keep her friends from the inevitable, but I had insisted on going ahead and meeting the right man. Now I could see how I liked it.

I drove home trying to remember whether or not you could learn from other people's experience. The hills were dark and fresh, and the road lonely and empty, save for the odd family of goats sleeping on a corner. The driveway to the house had been reduced to a track during the last rains, and it was evident from the grass that no vehicle had passed over it since I'd left. I wanted to write to the agent and ask for some money to fix the road, but then I didn't want to remind him that I was still in the house, paying a third of the rent.

Louise and the children came running out to meet me, and tell me all the news. There had been cows in the garden, Lawrence had been in a fight, all kinds of things had happened. Where had I been for four days?

I opened up the house and moved the chairs out on to the verandah again. Louise stood there talking to me, and I relaxed to hear problems that weren't my own, weren't relevant in any way – the teacher at the primary school had confiscated a geometry set, the children had acquired a kitten that peed on the bed, shoes were needed for Angeline, there were weevils in the flour bin. When she went off, I sat there and breathed the free air of a mountain top. There was nothing to be unhappy about at the Porters', nothing at all.

Carla

Katherine was on site when Bob came back. She said she was tired of driving back to Kingston, and then up into the hills every evening, so she was staying down there in some villa belonging to a friend of Richard's. Rose was with her and half of their office was camped in the living room. Once there was a place to stay, with a beach and a pool, suddenly everyone realised how important they were to the spa project and went to Portland to help out.

Bob came to see me at the office, and totally disconcerted me by walking in while I was on the phone to my brother. He was distressed. Apparently Katherine's tears and his absence had given people at her office the impression that they had broken up, and he had gotten a very offhand reception. Katherine had left for Portland without telling him – he had been calling her office every day from the States trying to reach her or Rose. Richard had actually taken his call once and advised him that he didn't appreciate people messing around with his friends, which, coming from Richard, could only be regarded as highly insulting.

I reminded Bob it was only a few months since he had been sitting there complaining about Katherine, and what had I told him then? You're on your own, my friend.

Bob shook his head, took off his glasses, wiped his face.

'What is it with you people? You're such smartasses. I get sick of it. Katherine has an answer for everything, and when she doesn't she damn well disappears. You sit there, you go out to lunch with us, you're such a big friend of Katherine's. You act like you think I'm the best thing that ever happened to her. And the first time there's a problem, you tell me, "You're on your own, you're on your own." Goddamn it, you've known this woman all your life. How come you can't help us out with each other? I'm sitting up there with my crazy wife telling me about how when we move back to America everything will be fine. Katherine's down here going nuts, thinking I'm going to leave her. She's gone off somewhere. Those assholes at her office won't tell me where she is. That asshole Richard tells me not to get excited. I'm not excited, I'm frustrated. I'm really angry.'

I twirled around in my chair a little, tidied up my desk. Thinking, you're not one of us. You're still on approval. If you were one of us you'd know better than to come whining to her friends. Who wants Katherine to go off with some old American who's going to be dead in five years? When she's young and should be enjoying life. Should be going around with a native, not an import. Should be over her wonderful Santo, that gave her the taste for old white men.

But, as I said, Bob was a very nice man. Could not be denied. Generous and funny, had time for everyone. So he wanted some time from me. I looked at him, pale from his two weeks away, a bit fatter from all the steaks and spaghetti and cream sauces he must have been eating. He was looking at the floor, trying to crush the arms of the chair with his hands.

'Well, she's staying down in Portland. Near the spa. But she'll be back at the weekend. I wouldn't advise you to go down there. She's working, and you haven't seen how those people get when they're having trouble on site. You better just wait till she comes. I don't know what to tell you, Bob. It just seems to me like you two have to decide what's going to happen. My opinion is that you and Sandy should pack up and go back to the States. Katherine will get over it.'

He gave me a depressed smile, as if he had expected nothing better from me but still had hoped for more, and stood up.

'Well, thanks a lot for everything, Carla. Let's hope we can all get over it. See you around.'

I immediately called the villa and left a message for Katherine to call me at home as soon as she came in. When she had left for Portland, she'd been perfectly calm. She said she'd had a bad few months but she was all right now, she had had time to think and get herself together. But with her, you never knew what all right meant. It could mean she'd decided to do something stupid and take the consequences, or that she'd hardened Bob out of her, or that she was temporarily OK.

I couldn't believe she had done something as malicious and selfish as to go away without leaving a message for Bob. He was not the kind of man who would appreciate that. It was pure malice, and he knew it, and he knew he had called her as often as he could, and he hadn't let one call end without telling her that he loved her and he was coming back. There was no cause to treat him like a fool, or a hard man. Bob was so soft with her, did whatever she wanted. He thought she felt the same way about him. It seemed unlikely to me. She was only soft in the head, her heart was Lord knows where.

When Katherine called me at home I told her what I thought of her tactics. She said she'd left a message for him with Richard, asking him to telephone her at the villa. She would call him at home now, and risk making problems for him with Sandy. She called me back ten minutes later. Bob was not in yet. Sandy had answered the telephone, and told her, 'I think it's time you stopped trying to separate me from my husband. I've given you plenty of time to do whatever you were going to do, and now I want it to stop. Do you understand me?'

Katherine had said, 'You're going to have to give us some more time.'

Sandy replied, 'I know my husband. Pretty soon you're going to find out what he's really like. I'll bet you won't like it at all.'

I didn't know Sandy. I'd met her once at some cocktail party, where she didn't know anyone and Bob had left her stranded by the trays of pepper shrimp. But she was evidently smart enough to know how to get to Katherine. Telling her that her suspicions about Bob were going to be shown to have steel foundations.

Katherine seemed to be taking it well. The week that she had stayed with me had been her bad time, seeing danger in every course, panicking about actually having to do something, decide something. She didn't know much about fighting, she was a master at defensive measures.

Anyway, a few days in Portland with Rose would give anyone a different perspective. Katherine said they had gone out at night and stopped for a drink in every bar between the villa and Port Antonio. They had been given a parrot, they had met a German comedian, they had been taken to dinner by the client and Katherine had rushed out and vomited lobster on to the terrace. Derek had come down one evening and fallen off a cliff during a moonlight walk with Rose. The only way she could have been enjoying herself more was if she had been up at her house with Bob.

Since there didn't appear to be much chance of that happening in the near future she'd decided to stay in Portland for a while and just talk to Bob by telephone. She was a coward, but I didn't blame her. Sandy might be American but there was no telling what she would do now.

Katherine

Bob called me at the villa and asked me to meet him for lunch in Port Antonio three days after he got back from Washington. He said Sandy had mentioned our conversation on the telephone and he thought we should talk about what was going on. Also he missed me. Didn't I miss him?

I didn't go to the site in the morning, but slept late. I called a bad hotel in Port Antonio, and booked a room in my name. Bob would have to pay for it if we used it, I couldn't afford it. I drove along the coast with my bathing suit under my dress and stopped at San San and swam by myself in the bay for at least an hour and a half. When I lived away from Jamaica I used to try to explain how it is to be able to stop your car on the way somewhere and swim in a cool turquoise sea. Of course there are lots of places where you can do that, but I only do it at home. Where I have a fair idea of the state of the water and the sharks and the possibilities of being accosted on the beach and the likelihood of being forgiven for arriving late with salt dusting every pore.

I wasn't late for meeting Bob. We met in the car park, and we went straight to the hotel and to bed which was the only place I could talk about Sandy. Or bear to listen to Bob talk about her, which was the way it was. He lay back and talked to someone – not me, I would never have involved myself in such a situation – about how life could be in Washington, with another woman, totally unlike me. He talked to me across his belly where I was resting my head, listening to his stomach object to the white rum and orange juice. I didn't listen to him really. There's no point when you don't

87

know what the person is talking about and you have no intention of asking.

At about two Bob decided that I should leave Sandy to him – her being his wife – and that we had to figure out our next move. It appeared that although he had a son by his first wife, and was very likely to be a grandfather soon, he felt he had missed out on children and wanted me to have some more. He hadn't had any children with Sandy because he had been building his business, and he'd persuaded Sandy she didn't want any either. Now this was the first thing I'd heard that needed my attention apart from the mutterings of my lover as we moved around the bed and prepared each other for pleasure everlasting. Little me's. Little him's.

I pushed him back on to the bed although we were getting dressed and we made love for the first time condom-free. On the way back I almost stopped for another swim before I remembered I was an engineer with a client and a spa to be built upon the rocks and the sea. To be calm is to be everything. Change should be like a spring entering a lake from way below the surface, and the monsters should be suspected but never seen. Having a child would change everything and nothing, make everything very different without moving me from the Porters', or from my job, or from my quiet place on the surface of the world. It was perfect. It made Bob everything without making him a problem. As I told Rose that evening at the villa, I didn't know why I hadn't thought of it before. She said, poor Bob. Poor man.

Carla

I started having problems in my office about the same time. Political problems. Some people started to think about the next election two years in advance, started to think about changes in government, different opportunities. It meant that some of the younger men in the office, the ones that mostly worried about their haircuts, and their shoes, and which of their girlfriends they would see tonight, began to notice that I kept myself very quiet and very busy and wondered what I was really doing all by myself in my office all day. I was lucky that their idea of screwing me up was to complain directly to our superiors about me. I knew I was covered in that direction, I was just worried about some obvious facts becoming generally known.

Anyway, Bob helped me out a lot with this. He told me he had a taste for outsmarting people. He advised me when it was appropriate to see no evil, hear no evil, speak no evil and when it was ncessary to make people think I was capable of going down the Grant's Pen Road and taking out a contract on them. He completely understood that I had had nothing to do with my brother getting permission to build a two-hundred-room hotel inside a designated nature reserve, and that people were just trying to give me problems.

He helped me because he thought I would help him with Katherine. Bob thought he wanted to leave his wife, but Katherine was an unsuitable woman to leave her for. He realised this when Katherine missed her first period within weeks of him coming back from America. He was thrilled until Katherine suggested that he should buy the Porters' house for her, preferably in cash, to ensure that she and the child had some security.

Now, I have to admit that I thought this was the first sensible move she'd made in a while. Property prices made it unlikely that Katherine could have afforded anything much, at her age and on her salary, but Bob had money to spare. And, as Rose pointed out, he didn't have much time to spend it. Sandy was handing out all kinds of information about his heart problems, the state of his liver, that his father had died of a heart attack at thirty, ditto his grandfather – it was a miracle that the man was still walking and talking.

Rose's attitude was a joke. On the one hand she kept warning Katherine not to do what she had done. She told her it was pure hard times trying to bring up a child without a 'man at yard'. On the other hand, she said money had been her main worry. If she hadn't had a mortgage she could have managed very well. She said Bob was always talking about spreading money around. Let him spread a little in Katherine's direction. He could afford a wife and a babymother, and therefore he should afford them. Rose and Sandy started having lunch together to pick each other's brains.

I was relieved that I didn't hear any more about love from Katherine, although I heard plenty of it from Bob. He was outraged at Katherine's suggestion, but he was outraged for so many reasons that it took him some time to settle on the main one. The main reason was that he intended to marry her. He intended to divorce Sandy and marry Katherine. Katherine's plan to be paid off for loving and childbearing with the Porters' house, free and clear, was the wrong plan. He expected a lot more. He wanted to give a great deal more. He suspected Richard, Katherine's boss, of having made the suggestion. He believed in Katherine 'not being like that'.

Katherine told me that, yes, in fact, she had discussed her pregnancy with Richard. After all, the relationship with Bob had crash-landed on to the level where Richard had all his experience. It hadn't exactly been Richard's idea. Richard had congratulated her on her foresight in becoming pregnant by a white American. This indicated that she was less stupid than she looked. Then he'd told her to go for marriage, and if she couldn't get that, she should ask for money. Katherine had decided to ask for the house all by herself.

At the time, I thought it was hilarious. It was interesting. Katherine called me almost every day with updates. She was fine, she was powerful, she was making up her mind. Bob came to see me to discuss my office politics, and then we would talk about Katherine. I liked him very much. He sat in my office and told me everything that he'd ever thought about her, how his feelings had changed, how he'd stopped escaping from being bored and lonely and wanted to make a new life with her. I told him that if he didn't marry Katherine he should definitely stay married to Sandy. I told him that every little thing would be all right.

Katherine invited me up to the Porters' for lunch one Saturday. Bob could no longer come up every weekend because he had to stay at home and discuss Katherine with Sandy. When I arrived there were still people drifting down the road from the house. Katherine was sitting on the verandah with her notebook where she wrote down all the requests for help.

'I don't know why you don't go into politics,' I said. 'Get paid for running around for these people.'

'Well, I can tell you it's difficult without Bob. He usually does half of the work.' She looked weary. We ate on the verandah as usual. I hated the house. It looked bare and ugly, and half the furniture was broken. She said she liked to have enough room to pace up and down. I asked her if Bob had agreed to buy it.

'Carla, the man wants me to marry him. He wants us to live in America. He doesn't like it here any more.'

'Well, what's wrong with America? Apart from them wanting you to work for your money?' We both laughed. I had a friend who had moved back home after two years in Miami, claiming that he had been expected to be at work every morning by nine, and work until five every afternoon. Without fail, Monday to Friday. Telling us about it he had kept repeating, 'Imagine! Every day! By nine!'

Katherine shook her head, 'That's what I keep trying to explain to Bob. Now that I've seen gay Paree, I just want to stay down on the farm. Can you see me in Washington, going to the shopping mall twice a day?'

I could, but I didn't say it.

'Well, I can see why you might not want to marry a man that treats his wife like Bob treats Sandy. On the other hand, you could end up with worse if you marry someone like Sam. The main thing is to keep him in Jamaica until you figure out exactly what you want.'

'At least another seven or eight months anyway.' Katherine smiled. 'We both want a girl.'

We walked around the huge garden. Most of it was just bush. I noticed that there would be plenty of space for a hotel – a mountain lodge with horse-riding and a few tennis courts. The view of the mountains was spectacular, although at night it would not look like much, with only a few lights from squatters making fires at the edge of the forest. I made the suggestion and, of course, she acted like I was crazy.

'I have enough problems, thank you. I can't believe the way you go around looking for deals the whole time. Give it a rest, Carla.'

'OK, relax. I just thought if you were going to make a deal with Bob on the house you could really develop something up here. Get Rose to design you a hotel, borrow some money, provide a few jobs for all your friends.'

No answer. Katherine walked away and started pulling leaves off a guava tree. You can't tell some people anything. Katherine, who hadn't even gone to tell Rat Man's parents 'Sorry', could get very mean about the idea that there wasn't a hair of difference between me and her and Rose. In my opinion, she was worse. Bob was a bad bargain but Katherine was not a great one herself.

I went down the hill, blowing my horn on every corner against the mad drivers that live in those parts.

Katherine

That June we had flood rains. The road up the hill came down at least twice a week. The PWD kept clearing away the landslides, but they didn't do anything about keeping the earth on the hillslopes. You could see the trees which leaned at a horizontal over the road, and steep banks held by nothing more than wynne grass, and spot the next landslide. I had the flu. Late for work one clear fresh morning, I raced down the hill and almost crushed three men who were helping to loot the Red Stripe truck which had turned over taking Deadman's Corner. People were running up the middle of the road carrying cases of beer, as gleeful as supermarket security guards after a hurricane has blown out the doors.

I didn't bother to try to get past the wreck. At home I was preparing to go back to bed when Louise came into the bedroom to empty the buckets under the main leaks. The Porters' house was porous to the last.

'Ma'am,' she said, 'I wondering if you could take me and the children to America, when you going with Mr Bob. I would really like to go and see how America look like.'

Bob had been up on Sunday and had spent a few minutes around the back of the house talking to Louise. I sat down on the bed, hating my belly.

'Louise, if I was going to America, of course, I would take you. But when the time comes to put down this load I'm going to be right here, same as usual, and you're going to be right here, washing nappies every day in life.'

She looked at her bare feet. 'Every day in life,' she repeated. 'So you not going to America for the baby?'

'Bob thinks I'm going to change my mind, but I'm not. If you want to do something, you should try to persuade Bob to buy this house for me, so that we'll all know where we're going to be living this time next year.'

Louise sucked her teeth and glared at me. 'Is dis ole' house you want? With dis roof? Ma'am, the way that man love you, I can't believe say you not going follow him go America. If it was me, I would gone long time.'

'You want to go to America, ask Bob to take you. I'm going to lie down now.'

I lay down. Louise left, pushing the bucket out of range of the leak with her foot, and I had to get up again and move it into place. She would hate it in Washington anyway.

My pregnancy had turned Bob into a man with one last chance. He was, alternately, loving and concerned, and the next day he would be a man from whom I was trying to steal a child. For myself, I hate things which can't be shovelled out of the way, or repaired with string.

Bob wouldn't stay in Jamaica because he had found out that it was a dangerous place to live for a man with smooth, soft flanks and no one to watch his back. He was the only man on the island who wasn't afraid of machine guns at 3.0 a.m., and neighbours screaming, 'Oh, Lord have mercy.' He was afraid of Rose when she told him that I wouldn't marry him because his liver was damaged, and of Richard when he explained I just wanted the house as evidence of good intention. He was afraid of people that didn't require guns to do mortal damage. He had walked out on Carla for laughing at him, and saying, 'Just figure out a way to outsmart her. Look on this as a business proposition.'

However it seemed he had decided to take her advice. I was always going to love him, but I wanted him to leave me alone to look out at the mountains and think about growing strawberries next year. I refused to think about anything else. With Bob, there would be world without end. American eternity, with life and liberty slipping away in the pursuit of happiness.

Louise and I could cope with a baby. Richard had promised me a big Christmas bonus. I was just having to learn to deal with going to my office every day, where everyone, from Richard to the messenger, was popping in to give me their thoughts on my impending marriage to Sandy's husband.

Sandy had a few thoughts on the matter as well. Rose, in her usual unbelievable fashion, thought that Sandy and I should get together to sort out Sandy's problem with Bob leaving her for me. Rose's long lunches with Sandy had convinced them both that direct negotiations were the best option. Direct negotiations between Sandy and me, that is. Bringing Bob into it might confuse the issue, since he persisted in thinking that his relations with wife and girlfriend were not only his business, but his responsibility. Rose thought that leaving these matters to Bob could only result in Sandy having to get a job and Katherine having to give up hers. Rose sat on my drafting stool speculating on endless cheerful possibilities, and refusing to let me pay any attention to my work.

I agreed to have lunch with Sandy, wanting to show that I could be an active participant in all the worry and excitement surrounding my private life. Rose came to hold my hand. She dressed up for it, and sat there, hardly breathing, listening to every word for future reference. We ate at the most expensive restaurant in Kingston, at Rose's expense. 'You don't want her to intimidate you with any crying or carrying on,' Rose said. 'She'll have to be nice with all her friends from the embassy at the next table.'

Sandy had got thinner, looked great, smiled her way across the restaurant, kissed my cheek before she sat down. I was preparing to cry at any moment. She did not even glance at the menu. She said that she had two children from a previous marriage. Did I know that? No, I didn't. I raised my eyebrows at Rose, but she hadn't known either. Sandy gave me a warm look, so understanding it might have been patronising. They lived in England with Sandy's ex-husband because Bob had needed so much time and attention for the first few years of their marriage. Did I know that? No, I didn't. Well, but then surely I could see that having given up her children for Bob, she wasn't prepared to lose him? Yes, I could understand that. Rose kicked me under the table. I was supposed to say that I was very sorry but I had my own life to lead.

I asked Sandy whether she knew that I didn't want to marry Bob. She folded her hands on the table and examined them. Yes, she knew. She thought it was very sensible. She knew that the girls down here had babies without caring whether or not they had a man around. She was still looking at her hands, and she missed Rose mouthing, 'Bitch!' at her. If I wanted Bob to buy me the Porters' house Sandy would do her best to make sure that he did. She would also press him for child support, and she thought it was possible that she could arrange for him to visit me and the baby, oh, say, twice a year. I said I thought Bob had the best of intentions and that he and I could come to some amicable agreement.

Sandy kissed me again, told me what a nice, pleasant girl I was, and would I mind if she didn't stay for lunch. When she was gone, Rose laughed. 'Bob seems like a man who always goes for the same kind of woman. You're the best, Katherine. I thought I was hard on the world, but you and Sandy really don't give room to move around.'

I cried and Rose had the lobster. I tried to remember what Bob had told me about Sandy. What kind of man would tell you his life story, and in such detail, and not mention that his wife had two children, Belinda and Alexander? Alive and well in Birmingham.

No one mentioned the lunch to Bob. Rose was too horrified, Sandy was too smart, and I was too guilty.

I told him Rose had given me some information. What about Belinda and Alexander? Bob smiled at me. 'Is that what you're worried about? I didn't tell you about them because I didn't want Sandy to come across like a total bitch. Like I was making excuses. She couldn't wait to dump those kids. She was dying to get back to the States and live it up in Washington with her new man. I didn't have much money then, but I had about ten times as good prospects as her first husband. She made the right choice. And you should too.'

'I thought you said you were sick of how cynical and manipulative we are down here in Jamaica. If that's not cynical, I don't know what is.'

Bob put his arms around me, and I could feel how safe he could make me. 'I thought you said you didn't want to know everything about me.'

'I don't.' I nestled my head on his chest. I wanted to choose what not to know.

Carla

I suppose that no one could fault Katherine for wanting a house and land more than she wanted a husband. People got angry because she wanted him to give her a house, but she didn't want to give him a place in it.

After the lunch with Sandy, the affair between Katherine and Bob became very troublesome for everyone. Rose and Sandy let people know that a deal had been made. The matter was resolved. But then Richard, at this late stage, decided that Katherine and Sandy had exceeded their authority, and started telephoning Bob to offer advice and support. When Richard changed sides, the office changed sides with him. Katherine walked into work one morning and not one person enquired whether she had vomited in the early hours. She was in my office by lunch-time, on the verge of weeping and wailing.

Up until that moment, she hadn't told me about the lunch with Sandy – although I had heard about it from Rose. As if Rose knew anything about property. I reminded Katherine that she only had one friend to consult when it came to matters of real estate, and that was me. She looked out of the window and kept repeating that she was relying on Sandy to help her sort things out. I considered her approach to be pure tomfoolery, given the size of the property and its potential, but she wasn't listening to me, she was trying to calm herself down.

While Katherine was sitting there complaining about how nobody understood that she did, in fact, love Bob, I rang Sandy at home. Sandy assured me that she had contacted the Porters and they had agreed to sell the house. What was holding everything up

99

was that Bob was acting like a wild man, and refusing to discuss the matter at all. She was wondering if I had any idea why Bob was behaving so unreasonably. The woman was completely serious.

I didn't have anything to say to her in any case. Bob had stopped coming to see me around the time he launched his campaign to marry Katherine, and I had just let him be. However when an article appeared in the newspaper by some botanist complaining about the species and habitats destroyed by my brother's hotel, I rang Bob to discuss it. He was out of the office and never called me back. That did annoy me. You can always make time to deal with business.

Katherine was seeing him every Sunday and a few times during the week. He was feeling old and tired. Apparently Sandy had succeeded in making him remember that he was going to die one day, and probably sooner rather than later. He found he was living to fulfil his obligations, but he was still objecting to meeting his obligations with cash.

What was there to say about Bob at this point? He had put an idea into Katherine's head, and here were the consequences, plain and simple. He wanted a baby by Katherine and he was going to get one. I think he was disoriented by how quickly everything was happening. He was rushing around fighting Katherine and Sandy's fixed positions, but he couldn't think of any acceptable alternatives.

The man remained very ignorant about Katherine. Deeply ignorant. Bob was trying to overcome Katherine's resistance to marriage, and in the meantime, Katherine was busy calculating the cost of repairs to the roof at the Porters', figuring out what percentage of her salary she could save every month if she wasn't paying rent, and how much she would have to invest to put five acres under coffee. She was busy behaving as though her welfare was paramount.

As I said, I didn't take sides. In fact, I didn't have time to keep up with every quarrel, insult, reconciliation. I had a survey done of the house and the land, and gave Sandy a price range for her negotiations with the Porters. I went with Katherine to Grand

Cayman for a weekend to stop her from having a nervous breakdown. I invited Bob to lunch sometimes, but he never came.

When Katherine was in her seventh month he came wandering into my office at five-thirty and asked me if I wanted to go and have a drink. The man was thin and burnt-up looking. He had been drying and leathering in the hot sun and salt water for over two years and he didn't look as if he had had any benefit from it.

We went to The Hi-Rise Dread where you could get organic callaloo patties with your vodka, and there was some sort of view and some type of breeze. Bob said it was his regular 'after work, half-way home' drinking place. We drank.

'Carla, I just wanted to thank you for not taking sides in this.'

I had nothing to say to that.

'I know you think I should just buy the house for Katherine and go back to Washington.'

'I never told you to buy any house for anybody.' I finished my drink. I would catch the worst of the traffic. Bob ordered me another vodka without asking if I wanted one. Since time was passing, I asked him what he wanted to talk about.

'I know you didn't just invite me for a drink. It must be months since I've seen you.'

'Well, I wanted to know why you're instructing my wife on the purchase of Katherine's house.' The old, cold Bob. He still hadn't figured out that that approach could not get him anywhere with me or with Katherine.

'I'm not instructing her. Real estate happens to be one of my areas of expertise. Just helping out a friend.'

'That's fine, Carla. Because if it's my money that's going to be used to buy something for my girlfriend, then I expect to be consulted.'

You see, that's how it goes when you get friendly with people like Bob. He could go from asking you, to telling you, in no time at all, depending on how hurt he was feeling. He was ripe and ready for someone to teach him some manners, but I had had a difficult week and didn't have the heart to do it. I just smiled and looked at his worn away face and let him explain his position. I don't even remember what he said, except that he was less angry and more

101

miserable than ever. I drank my vodka and felt glad not to be in the middle of it. Nothing is more stale than trouble between a man and a woman. The bar closed at midnight and Bob stopped talking long enough for me to get to my car.

That was really the last time I spent with him until the baby was born. After drinking with me that night, he became rather bitter and resigned. He asked Sandy for a divorce but kept living in the same Poinciana townhouse with her. He bought the Porters' house but fought with Katherine for two weeks over whether both their names, or only her name, would be on the deeds. Yes, I felt for that man.

The defeat was on his face when they gave him his daughter to hold at the hospital. Of course we had all gone there, to be in at the kill – me, Richard, Rose, Sandy, Louise. We watched him kiss the child and demonstrate his surrender by turning to ask Katherine what surname was on the birth certificate. The baby had his names, first and last, but on the relevant line Katherine had written Father Unknown. In case, she had told me, of custody proceedings somewhere down the line. We all stood around, looking at the child and drinking, and Bob watched Katherine lying in the bed, as though the baby, or maybe even the champagne, might do something, change something, heal something.

Katherine

At about nine o'clock that evening I heard people coming up the drive. It was like the night when Rat Man was killed. The baby was asleep. I locked the door of her room, and then unlocked it – in case the house was going to be burnt or something. I picked her up and carried her round to the front of the house. Her father wasn't here, but here was Lloyd, and the little boy being carried by a big man I didn't know, and five or six other women and men. Here was Louise coming around the corner of the house, and greeting people.

'Good evening. Is he all right?' I asked the man with the boy.

'No, ma'am. Look like something burs' inside him. We have to carry him go hospital.'

'I tried to find him.'

The boy was unconscious, and his eyes rolled. I saw the women watching me. They were prepared for me if I failed to show regret. Lloyd grasped my shoulder.

'A' tell them, ma'am. A' tell them you would never go and leave him. And is so the boy tell them. Him did 'fraid say he damage the car. Him feel say he going get a beating.'

Louise, who hadn't been told about the accident, suddenly screamed at them, 'What kind of ras' ignorance is that? She going beat him? For what? What kind of damn ignorance you coming here with?'

None of them said anything, just looked at me with hard, expectant faces, ignored Louise. I handed Roberta to Lloyd, who took her with the tenderness of a father.

'Let me go and get my car keys. We'll take him to Casualty at the University.'

When I came running back they were standing around the car talking to Louise, who was still shrieking about ignorance. One of the women said that she wanted to come, it was her sister's boy, after all. She and the father, holding the child, eased into the back seat, and Lloyd came in front with Roberta. I asked Louise to give the others something to drink and they could wait until we came back. Two of the men ran down the driveway alongside the car until I speeded up and left them behind.

I wanted to drive fast for the boy who had been hurt for three hours, but I didn't want them to think it had happened because I was reckless. The familiar corners appeared in the dark and vanished into the dark. Going across the bridge into Gordon Town, Lloyd quieted Roberta who had finally woken up.

'Glad to see you still with us, ma'am,' he said. 'I glad to see you buy that house from those people, and staying up here with us in the hills.'

'Well, I can't leave the mountains. Try my best, but I can't leave them.'

At the hospital they took the boy into Casualty and I stood around for a little, being necessarily officious, and insisting to the doctor in my BMW voice, that this was no ordinary child off the street, not just another Friday night accident. They took him into surgery. I looked at the wounded people coming in on stretchers and decided to wait in the car with Lloyd. We had agreed to spend the night at the hospital and wait for news.

The sky was very clear over the mountains circling the city, and cloudy over the amphitheatre where Kingston played. I took Roberta from Lloyd and made faces at her outraged cries.

'When she father coming? Is long time I don't see him,' Lloyd asked, stroking the baby's flailing hands.

'He's gone back to live in America. But he's coming for a visit soon. I'll bring him to see you when he comes.'

If, and when. If Bob forgives me, and when he can bear to drive up into the hills again, where we're all going along, very much as before.

THE CARIBBEAN WRITERS SERIES

The book you have been reading is part of Heinemann's long-established Caribbean Writers Series. Details of some of the other titles available are listed below, but for a catalogue giving information on the whole series, and on the African Writers Series write to:
for UK customers: Heinemann Educational,
Halley Court, Jordan Hill, Oxford OX2 8EJ, UK.
For US customers: Heinemann Inc, 361 Hanover Street,
Portsmouth, NH 3801-3959, USA;

CLEM MAHARAJ
The Dispossessed

The history of Highlands, a sugar estate, is bound up with the lives of the poor people who live and labour on it. Clem Maharaj brings a delicate clarity to his heartfelt description of these workers.

IAN McDONALD
The Humming-Bird Tree

Alan lives in comfort with his parents in 1940s Trinidad. When he becomes friends with the East Indian servants, his parents intervene. *The Humming-Bird Tree* is now a BBC film.

IAN McDONALD & STEWART BROWN (EDS)
The Heinemann Book of Caribbean Poetry

In a collection that celebrates the richness of the Caribbean, editors Stewart Brown and Ian McDonald offer the best of the new work being produced in English in the region, together with the finest poetry of an earlier generation of Caribbean writers. The anthology features such well-known names as Derek Walcott, Louise Bennett and Andrew Salkey, as well as younger poets such as David Dabydeen and Jean Binta Breeze.

FRANK COLLYMORE
The Man Who Loved Attending Funerals and Other Stories
(With an afterword by Harold Barratt)

An engaging collection of shorter fiction by this multi-talented
Barbadian. The title story depicts a man who revels in ritual at
the burials of acquaintances, and has to recognise his own
mortality.

LAWRENCE SCOTT
Witchbroom

Lavren Monagas de los Macajuelos pours forth epic and
intimate tales of conquest, crime and passion. As this
extraordinary hermaphrodite character both observes and acts
in the unfolding drama, we are drawn into his/her account of
the quest for El Dorado. The stories are told in the traditional
Caribbean style of irony – *mamaguy*.